STRANDED
WITH HER
GREEK TYCOON

STRANDED WITH HER GREEK TYCOON

KANDY SHEPHERD

MILLS & BOON

First published in Great Britain 2018
by Mills & Boon, an imprint of HarperCollins*Publishers*
1 London Bridge Street, London, SE1 9GF

Large Print edition 2018

© 2018 Kandy Shepherd

ISBN: 978-0-263-07383-6

MIX
Paper from
responsible sources
FSC™ C007454

This book is produced from independently certified
FSC™ paper to ensure responsible forest management.
For more information visit www.harpercollins.co.uk/green.

Printed and bound in Great Britain
by CPI Group (UK) Ltd, Croydon, CR0 4YY

To my dear friend Anne Yeates and her clever boys, for introducing me to the historic university town of Durham in Northern England—the inspiration for my hero and heroine's past.

CHAPTER ONE

CRISTOS THEOFANIS HAD made such a monumental mess of his own marriage, he found it impossible to share in the joy as he watched his favourite cousin and his wife renew their wedding vows. Seeing their happiness in each other, the intimate smiles shared by a man and a woman deeply in love, made him fist his hands at the memories of what he had lost.

But he was careful to keep in place the mask he chose to present to the world—happy, without-a-care Cristos, unaffected by the losses that secretly haunted him. His pain was his own to keep all to himself.

The renewal ceremony had been held in the tiny white chapel perched on the edge of a cliff overlooking the turquoise waters of the Ionian sea on his cousin's privately owned island of Kosmimo. Now the happy couple was flocked by joyous well-wishers as they spilled out of the chapel.

Cristos stood alone by a stunted cypress tree, marooned on his own black cloud of dark thoughts, his face aching from the effort of forcing smiles he didn't feel.

Of course he wished his cousin well, but Cristos was haunted by memories of his own wedding five years ago in a register office in the medieval city of Durham in the north of England. He had looked down at Hayley, his bride, with pride and adoration and a wondering disbelief that such an amazing woman had agreed to share her life with him. In return, her eyes had shone with love and trust as she'd offered him both her body and, more importantly, her heart. A priceless gift. *One that had been wrenched away from him.*

Remorse tore through him like a physical pain. He had not seen his wife in more than two years. Two years and five months to be precise. He could probably estimate the time in hours, minutes even. For every second of that separation he had torn himself apart with self-recrimination and guilt. Now, he didn't even know where Hayley lived, what she was doing. He had hurt her by not being there when she'd needed him. But she hadn't given him a chance to make it up to her.

With a ruthlessness he had not believed his sweet, gentle wife had possessed, she had left him and completely deleted him from her life.

As his cousin Alex and his wife Dell kissed to the sound of exuberant cheering, Cristos closed his eyes as he remembered the joy of kissing Hayley when the celebrant had told him he could claim his bride. They had been as happy as these two. Excited about the prospect of a lifetime together. Deliriously in love. Confident that all they'd needed was each other when the world had seemed against them.

'We were once just like them.' The words were no more than a broken murmur, as light and insubstantial as the breeze playing with the branches of the tree above him.

Cristos's eyes flew open in shock at the wistful tones of a once familiar voice. *Hayley.* From somewhere below his shoulder, where she'd used to fit so neatly, he seemed to breathe in the elusive hint of her scent. Crazed by regret, he must be conjuring up a ghost from his past.

He turned his head. His heart jolted so hard against his ribs he gasped. She stood there beside him, looking straight ahead towards the church, not up at him, as if she couldn't bear to meet his gaze. *His wife.*

He put out his hand to touch her, to make sure he was not hallucinating. Her cheek was soft and cool and very, very real. 'It's you, *koukla mou,*' he said, his voice hoarse. He had not used that term of endearment for years—it belonged to her and her only.

Immediately he regretted his words. Drew back his hand. He had loved her unconditionally but she had thrown that love back at him. Yes, he had made mistakes he deeply regretted. But she had not given him the chance to remedy them. She had hurt him. Humiliated him. Put him through hell as he'd searched Europe for her. But she hadn't wanted to be found.

'Don't call me that,' she said. 'I'm not your little doll or your gorgeous girl or whatever that word translates to. Not any more.'

'Of course you're not,' he said tersely.

Her gaze flickered away from him and she bit her lower lip with her front teeth as she always did when she was nervous. Or dreading something. *What was she doing here?*

He stared at her, still scarcely able to believe she

was real. Hungry, in spite of himself, for every detail of her appearance. She was wrapped against the late morning February chill in slim trousers and an elegant pale blue coat he had once bought for her from a designer in Milan. The coat, belted around her narrow waist, was the same but he was shocked to see Hayley was not. The image of her he had for so long held in his mind shimmered around the edges and reformed into a different version of his wife.

Her beautiful blonde hair that had tumbled around her shoulders in lush waves was gone, shorn into an abbreviated pixie cut. *Like a boy* was his first dismayed thought. He had loved her long hair, loved running his hands through it, tugging it back to tilt her head up for his kiss. But a deeper inspection made him appreciate how intensely feminine the new style was, feathered around her face, clinging to the slender column of her neck. Her features seemed to come into sharper focus, her cheekbones appeared more sculpted, her chin more determined. Her youthful English rose prettiness that had so attracted him had, at twenty-seven, bloomed into an even more enticing beauty.

'Where the hell have you been?' he said. 'What are you doing here after all this time?'

She met his gaze. 'To see you. What else?'

Hope that she might be there to—at last—explain why she had abandoned their marriage roared to life only to be beaten back down by the cool indifference of her blue eyes, the tight set of her mouth. He wanted to demand that she explain herself. *She was still his legal wife.* But there was a barely restrained skittishness about her that made him hold back. He couldn't risk her running away from him again. *He wanted answers.*

She looked over to the gathering outside the church and then back to him. 'I didn't know your entire family would be here or I certainly wouldn't have come to this island,' she said.

There was something different about her voice. A trace of some kind of accent blurring the precise Englishness of her words. He was fluent in English and Italian, with passable French and Spanish, but he couldn't place it. *Where had she been?*

'This is a private function.'

'I would never have been on the guest list,' she said, a bitter undertone to her voice.

He was unable to refute the truth of her words. His family—in particular the grandmother who had raised him since he was fourteen—had disapproved of his marriage to Hayley and made no secret of it. For *Yia-yia* Penelope their union had been too rushed, too impulsive, too reminiscent of his own parents' hasty marriage that had brought the family so much grief.

'I want to know why you're here,' he said. 'The last time we met you told me you hated me. And then nothing.'

He didn't hate her, though there had been moments when he had wanted to. Since that day in the hospital in Milan when she had turned away from him, her face as pale as the hospital pillow, his emotions had gone from guilt for his neglect, to terror for her safety, through smouldering anger that she had thought so little of their marriage—*of him*—to wipe him without explanation from her life. Finally his anger had mellowed to a determined indifference.

Hayley made no reply. She placed great store on honesty. A shudder of foreboding made Cristos think her unexpected visit was not something he should be glad about.

'How did you get here?' Kosmimo was only accessible by boat. Or the helicopters of the wealthy guests who frequented the luxury retreat spa his hotelier cousin Alex had established on the island.

'I'd heard you were back in Nidri, staying with your grandparents.' His grandparents ran a tourist villa complex in the port town on the nearby island of Lefkada. 'Their maid told me you were here. I hired a man and his boat to bring me over.'

There'd been storms and the water was choppy. 'What man?' he said too quickly, too possessively. He wouldn't trust his wife to just anyone on these waters. Mentally he slammed a fist against his forehead. *She was no longer his concern.* Who knew what risks she'd taken in the last two years and five months without him to look out for her? More to the point, why should he care?

Her eyes narrowed at his tone. But she named a local boatman he knew well. 'Good choice,' he said.

Why had he doubted her ability to choose a safe boat ride? Hayley had always been practical, seeing a problem and finding a solution. Then she'd seen him as a problem and the solution as leaving him.

He looked over her shoulder, aware they had become the target of curious glances. Most of the people gathered here for the ceremony had never met Hayley. But he sensed their interest like a current buzzing through the congregation. Those in ignorance would very soon be made aware that this lovely blonde woman was Cristos's estranged wife. The one who had humiliated a Greek husband in a way a Greek husband should never be humiliated.

He shifted his body to shield her from curious gazes. That was all he'd ever wanted to do—protect her and look after her. Yet when she'd really needed him, he'd let her down so badly she had been unable to forgive him. Deep down, he had been unable to forgive himself.

'Why didn't you tell me you were coming?' he said, keeping his voice low.

'I wanted to see you face to face. But I wasn't sure you'd welcome me if I warned you.'

Banked up from years of frustration his words flooded out. 'Of course I'd want to see you. I need to know what happened. You left the hospital without telling me where you were going. I tried to find you. Your parents wouldn't tell me where you were. Or your friends. Your sister slammed the door in my face.'

She put her hand up to stop him. He noticed it wasn't quite steady. 'Stop. Not here. Not with an audience. What I have to say should be said in private. It's why I had to see you in person rather than—'

'Just say it,' he said through gritted teeth.

She played with the strap of her designer hand-bag—another gift from him—twisting it until he thought it would snap. Then she looked up at him. 'I want a divorce.'

He glared at her. 'The sooner the better,' he said.

Hayley took a step back and looked up at her soon-to-be-ex-husband. *Why, oh, why had she come here?* She'd thought she could handle see-ing Cristos again. In light of the love they'd once shared, surely it was the right thing to deliver the divorce papers in person rather than have them served on him by her lawyer?

But the moment she'd seen him standing under that tree in his dark coat staring moodily out to sea, she'd known it was a mistake. She'd been slammed by her impossible attraction to him with such force she'd had to plant her booted feet on the ground to keep herself steady. Dry-mouthed, heart pounding, she'd been unable to do anything but stare at him, stricken with hopeless longing.

He was now twenty-nine, and still the most beautiful man she'd ever seen. Perhaps *beautiful* wasn't the right word. But handsome, good-looking, striking, even *gorgeous* were not adjectives enough. Not for this man. Not for six feet two of broad-shouldered, narrow-hipped masculine perfection. Not for thick black hair, smooth olive skin that was a delight under a woman's stroking fingers, the surprise of pure green eyes.

Cristos could have modelled for the marble statues of the ancient Greek gods she had admired in Athens on their honeymoon. Instead just six months later, on a weekend break in London, he'd been scouted by an international model agency. As a macho Greek male, he'd scorned the idea. But they'd needed money badly and she'd talked him into at least trying it. He'd been booked for a prestigious job the first day he'd reluctantly signed the agency contract.

That was when she'd begun to lose him, Hayley reflected now, when he'd started to slip slowly away into a world that'd had no place for her. Pushing him into it was the stupidest thing she'd ever done. She had become the insignificant peahen to the glorious peacock of her magnificent husband. And he had allowed it to happen. He had left her alone to tend the nest while he strode with masculine insouciance the catwalks of the fashion capitals of Europe, shot advertising campaigns and commercials, all the while hobnobbing with the wealthy and well-connected. Every time she'd questioned him, he'd told her everything he did was for her and their financial security. For a while she'd believed him. Before she began to doubt him.

She gritted her teeth. The longing that surged through her wasn't for *this* Cristos. It was for the Cristos she'd fallen in love with as a student back in that pub in Durham when she'd been barely twenty-two. After her gap year, she was a year older than most of the people in her class and something about the group of older students had caught her attention. He'd been laughing with some fellow exchange students. The flash of his white teeth against his olive skin, the humour in those amazing green eyes had caught her attention then mesmerised her. He'd looked across to her and their gazes had connected. For a long moment there had been nothing—*no one*—else but him. The sounds of the pub had receded, the chatter and the clinking of glasses, until it had just been her and him, drinking in each other's eyes, their souls connecting. Or that was how it had seemed. Then his brow had furrowed in a quizzical frown. He'd put down his glass and left his friends behind to make his way to her side.

Even back then he'd been good at masking his feelings—she hadn't known for days he'd been as instantly smitten by her as she'd been by him. It was an attribute that had served him well in his unexpected new career. He'd easily been able to slip into the varied persona required of him as a successful male model. Smouldering and sophisticated in a tuxedo, or sporty and athletic on a yacht, he'd always looked the part on billboards all over Europe.

He'd got so good at donning those masks that towards the end she'd begun to wonder had she ever seen the true Cristos. But at the word 'divorce' his mask slipped and the raw anguish that momentarily darkened his eyes made her heart skip a beat. But it was gone so quickly she might have imagined it.

'Nothing about where you've been, what you've been doing—all you want to do is demand a divorce,' he said in a forced, neutral tone. But the tension in his jaw, the shadow in his eyes told her he wasn't as cool about it as he appeared.

She swallowed hard. 'It can't come as a surprise. We've been separated for two and a half years. That's more than enough grounds to dissolve our marriage.'

'So my lawyer told me when I instructed him to instigate proceedings two years after your desertion. The separation was proof the marriage had irretrievably broken down. That's all that's required.'

His words sounded so grim, so final. The excitement and passion of their early years together had disintegrated into disillusionment. Yet now, just looking at her husband made her remember exactly why she'd defied her family to marry him, given up her own dreams to let him follow his. But that was yesterday. She had to be strong. Good sex and fun weren't enough to build a lifetime on. She'd learned that on a heart-wrenching night in Milan two and a half years ago, alone in a hospital in a country where she didn't speak the language as she'd miscarried in pain and anguish, tears streaming down her face for all she had lost.

She cleared her throat. Although she'd practised the words over and over, they didn't come easily. 'I want to be free, to perhaps marry again one day.'

His mouth set in a tight line. 'Is there someone else?'

'He's just a friend at this stage.'

Steady, reliable Tim, as different from Cristos as it was possible for a man to be. There had not been one word of romance expressed between them but Hayley had sensed Tim wanted to grow the friendship into something more. She wanted security, stability, not the tumult her life with Cristos had been.

'Where did you meet this man?'

'In Sydney. But he's not—'

'You've been living in Australia?' He hissed a string of curse words in Greek. During their time together she'd worked to learn his language, but he'd refused to teach her the curses—such lan-

guage was not befitting his wife. If he only knew
it was nothing to what she heard in her job as a
mechanical engineer—a woman in what was still
essentially a man's world.

'I didn't think to look for you in Australia, of
all places,' he said.

'That's what I thought,' she said. 'It was as far
away from you as I believed I could get. I have
an aunt there. My parents arranged it.'

He was silent for a long moment as he looked
down at her, searching her face. 'Did I hurt you
that badly?' His voice was low and hoarse.

She nodded, too choked to risk attempting to
speak.

His words sounded as though they were being
torn from him. 'So many times I've regretted the
way I left you alone that day, that I wasn't there
when you needed me. I—'

Hayley had tried to block that final scene with
him from her memory; it was too painful to revisit. She put up her hand to stop him. 'I don't
want to hear this,' she said.

His dark brows drew together. 'Like you didn't
want to hear it then. You wouldn't let me explain
or try to make it up to you. You were hurting but

so was I and you kicked me to the kerb. Then left me and ran so far away I couldn't find you. After all we'd gone through together you did that. Now you show up out of the blue, crash my family's party and—'

'Please. I don't want to go there. It's over.' Her voice broke. 'I just want a divorce. That's the only reason I'm here.'

'You could have had divorce papers served on me from Australia. Notified me where you were so my lawyer could be in touch with yours. You shouldn't be here, Hayley.'

He turned from her, slanted his broad shoulders away so she once more could see the happy gathering outside the church doors.

'I hope I'm not intruding on a special family occasion,' she said a little stiffly. His family had hardly been what you would call welcoming to Cristos's young English bride the one and only time she had met them. His cousin Alex had been the exception.

'Alex and his Australian wife, Dell, are renewing their wedding vows. It's a special day for them, a gathering only for family and close friends.' His tone let her know she was now point-edly excluded from those categories.

'Your grandmother's maid told me. She said they'd only been married two years ago. I'm glad he found someone after the horror he went through.'

Alex's then fiancée had been killed in a hos-tage situation. It had made the news all around the world. 'We're all grateful to Dell,' Cristos said. The wife who had been accepted by the family, as opposed to Hayley, the unwelcome one.

She knew she didn't have the right to access his family news but she was curious. 'Why are they renewing their vows so soon? Isn't it usually older people who do that?'

'They had to get married in a hurry because their daughter Litza was on the way. Dell wanted to affirm their vows in a more relaxed manner.'

She looked towards the couple. 'Oh. That must be their little girl with Alex.' The red-haired cherub was gurgling with laughter. 'And Dell has a baby in her arms who looks just like a tiny Alex.' Hayley forced her voice into neutral. She didn't trust it not to quiver when she talked about babies. Especially to Cristos.

Hayley actually knew quite a lot about Alex and Dell. She'd been dismayed when she'd got all the way to Sydney to find even there she couldn't escape Cristos's family. Alex had been Australian born and a hospitality tycoon. His relocating to Greece after his tragic loss and finding happiness with Dell was ongoing fodder for the press.

'Their son, Georgios. He was born just a year after Litza.'

Hayley couldn't meet his eyes. The tension between them must be palpable. Their baby would have been just a little older than the little girl being proudly held by Alex if she hadn't miscarried that terrible night. But she couldn't, *wouldn't* talk about that. Strained silence from Cristos told her he couldn't either.

The breeze had picked up. She shivered and huddled deeper into her coat—the beautiful, expensive coat Cristos had given her out of guilt for one of his lengthy absences. 'I've come from a hot Sydney summer. It's freezing here. Not at all how I imagined an idyllic Greek island. I mean, it's beautiful but so chilly. Why did they choose to renew their vows in winter?'

'Alex and Dell wanted to have the ceremony

here in the chapel where they got married. The resort is fully booked out all through the warmer months. In summer they would not have had the privacy they wanted.'

She looked over to the group outside the chapel. 'I'm happy for them,' she said. 'I liked Alex when I met him and Dell looks lovely.'

'You weren't invited but he'll be glad to see you. And Dell must be dying to be introduced.'

Hayley took an abrupt step back. 'No! I've come to talk to you about the divorce and then go. The boat is waiting to take me back to Nidri.'

Cristos closed the gap between them with one long stride. 'You can't do that.'

'What do you mean?' He was too close. This close she was too aware of his warmth, his scent, his strength.

'I can't allow you to disrupt this special day.'

'That was not my intention,' she said. 'I just—'

He spoke over her, his tone low and urgent. 'Alex and Dell have been through more than you know. Allow them their day of celebrating their commitment to each other. Your abrupt departure would cause even more speculation than your arrival and put the focus on us instead of them. That wouldn't be fair. You've turned up here uninvited. But you are still legally my wife. Despite our separation, it would be expected that you would greet Alex and Dell and congratulate them. I'm asking you to do the right thing.'

Why did he have to put it like that—appealing to her innate sense of justice? 'I suppose I could say hello,' she said tentatively. Although it would take a monumental effort to congratulate the happy couple on their successful marriage while her own was in its death throes. 'It wouldn't take long to chat with them and then slip away to the boat.'

Cristos shook his head. 'That would cause even more disruption than if you left right now. There is to be a lunch at the resort. Stay here for that. Surely we can be civil to each other. But don't mention the divorce to anyone. It's none of their business. Let people think we are discussing reconciliation. Just until the party is over and you can leave with the other guests.'

She frowned. 'You mean pretend I'm still your wife?'

He shrugged. 'If you put it that way. Just for a few hours. Legally you *are* still my wife.'

'You mean I'd have to act loving and—?' Her breath started to come in tight gasps at the thought of it and she had to put her hand to her chest.

'Just civil would do, if you find the thought of pretending an affection you no longer feel so distressing,' he said. 'Just keep it dignified. You've caused me enough humiliation.'

'I don't know that I could face explanations and—'

'No explanations would be required. I have told my family nothing of what happened between us.'

And, no doubt, his relatives had assigned all the blame for the end of their union to her. Slowly, she shook her head, forced her breathing to return to something resembling normality. 'I'm sorry but I can't do it.' Such a charade would bring back old memories, old feelings she had fought so hard to put behind her.

He frowned his displeasure. 'Do it for my cousin's sake who liked you and stood up for you. Don't let us ruin this day for them.'

Us. How thrilled she'd been when they'd become a couple. How she'd loved to drop those magical words *we* and *us* into the conversation, preferably while flashing her engagement ring at the same time. Now Cristos used the word in such a different context it made her shudder. *Us* united in a charade of dishonesty. Although, she was forced to admit, it would be with the best of intentions and just for a few hours. She sighed out loud. He still knew which of her buttons to press. The last thing she'd ever want to do was ruin someone else's hard-won happiness. Everyone in Sydney knew the tragedy Alex had gone through.

She looked up at Cristos. At that handsome, handsome face that had once been so beloved. 'I'll do it. Then after lunch I'm out of here. With the divorce papers signed.'

And she would say goodbye to her husband for the very last time.

CHAPTER TWO

CRISTOS FISTED HIS hands by his sides. He could lie to himself all he liked but his indifference towards his wife was just another mask. Seeing Hayley again had stripped it away, leaving raw the ache for her he had never been able to suppress.

Call it desire, need, obsession—when she had first smiled at him across that crowded pub in Durham it had lodged in his heart like an arrow from Eros, the ancient Greek god of love and desire. He had found it impossible to wrench it out—even when he had tried to hate her for the way she had left him.

What he had felt for her defied logic, reason, common sense. But it hadn't been enough to see them through the loss of their baby, a time that should have brought husband and wife closer together in a shared grief rather than driven them inexplicably apart. *What had gone wrong?* He needed answers. And he had to get them from Hayley before she took that boat back to Nidri.

Of course, it wasn't as simple as that. Hayley had barricades up around her that might be impenetrable. But Cristos was an optimist. To be a successful gambler you *had* to be an optimist. And he was a gambler. His was not the kind of reckless, addictive gambling that had driven his late father to embezzlement and fraud and stints in prison. Not to mention unending shame for his mother's family.

Cristos's gambling took the form of calculated business risks that had led him to invest in start-up internet businesses—most of which had succeeded beyond all expectations. At not yet thirty, he was a multimillionaire. These days the wide spread of his investment portfolio ensured his fortune was secure—and kept growing. Yet he kept the gambler aspect of him a secret from his family. And had never shared it with Hayley.

His father had died when he'd been thirteen, followed six months later by the death of his mother. His grandparents had brought him back to Nidri, aged fourteen, to live with them. He'd been embraced with love by his grandparents and extended family. But he'd soon become uncomfortably aware of how closely he was scrutinised.

He looked so like his father that his family were terrified he had inherited his nature as well as his good looks. It felt as if they were always waiting to pounce and stamp out any undesirable traits. As soon as he'd realised that, he'd become adept at masking his feelings, hiding his true risk-taking self. It was allowed to come out only when he played football where a winner-takes-all attitude was encouraged.

He had started investing in a small way in app developments by his fellow students at university but had kept both his successes and failures well hidden. Even though he saw himself as a canny businessman, he could never admit to his worried grandparents that he could be in any way like his father, the man they blamed for the death of his mother, their only daughter. The secrecy had become a habit, another mask he was beginning to weary of wearing.

But optimism was all he felt now as he looked down into Hayley's face—a face he had doubted he would ever see again. It was difficult to stop himself from glancing at her every few seconds just to reassure himself she was really there. The sheen of her hair, the blue of her eyes, the curve of her mouth. She was here with him, in the same country, by his side. They were headed for divorce. But he intended to make the most of the hours ahead to get answers to the questions that had plagued him. Then he could put her firmly in the past and move on without being haunted by guilt or bitterness.

That was a much better position than he could have dreamed he'd be in when he'd thought back to their wedding this morning.

'Alex is looking our way. Let's go say hi,' he said. It seemed natural to reach for her, to fold her much smaller hand in his for the first time in years. But she stiffened against him.

Did she hate him so much she couldn't bear the most simple of touches?

'You agreed to do this—we have to make it look believable,' he said in a gruff undertone intended only for her.

He could tell the effort it took for her to release the tension from her body. 'I guess so,' she said, expelling a sigh.

She left her hand in his as he led her towards

the chapel but there was no answering pressure, no entwining of her fingers through his. Their linked hands were purely for appearances' sake. But it signalled they were together—for today at least. The fewer questions his family had about her sudden appearance, the better. They would take their cues from him. If he appeared unperturbed they would not question what Hayley was doing here.

His cousin and his wife had been posing for photos with their children but had now handed them over to their doting grandmothers. Cristos was glad. He would find it impossible to keep his mask in place if he had to watch Hayley react to the children, knowing how much she had wanted the baby they had lost that terrible night in Milan. The night that was branded on his memory for ever, to be brought out and poked and prodded in an agony of self-recrimination for failing her. But there had also been fault on her part. He had wanted the baby, but she had not allowed him to share her grief—let alone acknowledge his.

He'd been in a business meeting—a meeting that had turned out to be pivotal to his rapid rise to riches. The deal he'd done that night had been a major step up to the fortune he had sought as security for his wife and the family they had wanted to raise together. He'd had his phone turned off. When he had switched it on it had been to find a series of messages from Hayley, escalating in urgency until the last one had said she was being taken by ambulance to hospital.

When he'd got there it had been too late. She had lost the baby. And he had very quickly realised he had lost his wife.

Now Alex and Dell stepped forward from their crowd of well-wishers to greet him and Hayley. He could tell Dell was bubbling over with curiosity about this unexpected visit from the wife she had never met but had heard so much about. He had to tamp down on his own curiosity at what his lovely wife had been up to since their split. Who was the man who had prompted her to seek a divorce? Jealousy, dark and invasive, roiled in his gut. It was an emotion relatively new to him. He had always felt certain of Hayley's fidelity. But he had spent the past two and a half years tormented by graphic imaginings of her in the arms of another man.

Alex gave Hayley a welcoming hug. But over

Hayley's shorn blonde head he questioned Cristos with his eyes: *What's going on?* Alex had become as close as a brother. They shared secrets. Cristos knew the truth behind his cousin's hasty marriage and Alex and Dell knew the extent of Cristos's fortune. Alex would be as surprised as he was by his wife's sudden reappearance.

'Where have you been hiding?' Alex asked Hayley, valiantly tiptoeing around the truth. Alex knew all about Cristos's fruitless search for her.

'Sydney,' Hayley said after hesitating a moment too long.

Alex's dark brows rose.

'I was living there for—'

Auburn-haired Dell interrupted. 'Sydney is my home town!' she exclaimed. 'I'd love to hear what you got up to there. Not only that, of course— I've been longing to meet you. Unfortunately we now have to go share ourselves around the other guests. But I'll seat you near us for lunch so we can chat.'

Her ebullient welcome defused the awkwardness of Hayley's surprise visit and Cristos shot his cousin's wife a glance of gratitude. He'd made friends with Dell when she had been working for

Alex on Kosmimo, before there had been any romance between her and his cousin. There had been no one more delighted when they'd got married and he'd been their best man. If Hayley and Dell hit it off it would help make the rest of the day go smoothly.

'I'll look forward to that,' Hayley said, returning Dell's smile—her smile was pointedly not directed at him. Dell hugged Hayley before she turned to move away.

That left just the two of them, standing apart from the other guests in the glorious but increasingly chilly grounds of the chapel. But Cristos didn't even notice the view of the white-capped sea or the profusion of dark clouds rolling in. His senses could only register the presence of his wife. Hayley might be hostile but she was *here*. Before she got back on that boat to Nidri he would insist he got answers.

But his spirits dipped as he noticed his seventy-seven-year-old grandmother heading their way. Hayley noticed too. He heard her dismay in a hiss of indrawn breath and she tensed as if to flee. 'I don't think I can handle a confrontation with your grandmother,' she said. 'That wasn't part of the deal.'

Cristos's protective instinct kicked in. He'd kept his anger about the ugly way Hayley had ended their marriage to himself. He would not tolerate criticism of her from anyone else. Not even his beloved grandmother, who had rather an impressive track record in that regard.

He put his arm around Hayley and drew her close. She did not object, realising, perhaps, that it would be easier if they gave the appearance of being a couple. 'Leave my grandmother to me,' he said.

Dell called Penelope the purveyor of information for the extended family—kind terminology to describe an unashamed gossip and self-appointed matchmaker. His *yia-yia* had worked to get Alex and Dell together despite seemingly impossible odds. But she was convinced Cristos had made completely the wrong match in Hayley. She'd made that very clear to Hayley the one time they'd met when he'd brought Hayley home to introduce her.

The old woman's journey towards them now was hindered by the other guests greeting her, but she would be with them in mere minutes. He could not allow old grievances to erupt that might make Hayley change her mind about staying for lunch. Not before he'd had time to thrash out the truth behind the reasons they had parted.

Hayley twisted within the protection of his arm to look up at him, her blue eyes clouded with concern. The wind lifted fine wisps of blonde hair that feathered around her face. He resisted the urge to smooth them into place. Such an intimate touch belonged to their past.

'Your grandmother hated me before. What will she think of me now?' she whispered.

'Hate?' He frowned. 'That's too strong a term. Penelope didn't approve of you—or me at the time, for that matter—but I'm sure she didn't hate you. We didn't ask their permission and married without inviting them to the wedding. That meant we broke all sorts of Greek family rules.'

Her mouth turned down. 'I didn't make it any better by telling her that my own parents weren't invited either. Your grandmother drew her own conclusions about that. Conclusions that didn't reflect well on me.'

'Remember your parents didn't approve of me

either. That was another reason we didn't tell any family about the wedding until we were Mr and Mrs.'

Hayley didn't deny it. 'They thought I was too young to get married. Especially while I was still at uni. My father was so disappointed in me.'

There had been more to it than that. 'They might have thought better of it if you'd married someone they approved of. Your mother was disappointed I was from humble origins.' Her mother had had a particular sneer for him that had let him know she'd thought her daughter had married way beneath her.

'That you were a foreigner was reason enough for her disapproval.' Was that a glimmer of a smile of complicity from his estranged wife, as the memories danced across her face? 'She saw it as an act of defiance on my part. To get married at the register office and have lunch afterwards at the pub with our friends. What a crime that was in "Surrey mother" circles.'

He smiled in return. 'We got married exactly the way we wanted. Free from anyone's expectations but our own. I never regretted that, in spite of the dramas it caused with my family.'

'Me neither,' she said. 'No matter how it turned out in the end.' Her gaze met his for a long moment. Then the shutters came down and she turned her face away. Why would she want to indulge in reminiscence about their wedding when she'd come seeking a divorce?

'Penelope is heading our way,' she said.

He felt a shiver run through her. 'Cold?' he asked. As the wind rose, the temperature was beginning to drop.

'A little scared, to be honest. Your grandma is a formidable lady. She doesn't look any less hostile than when she interrogated me the first time we met when we came to Greece on our honeymoon.'

'Which is why we never came to the islands again.' His family's rejection of his wife had hurt Hayley so much he had decided to give his grandparents time to get used to the idea of his marriage before they met again. Then when the modelling career he had fallen into so reluctantly had taken off with such speed there hadn't been the chance to come back, to try and mend bridges. Or, indeed, time to work on the cracks that had been appearing in his marriage that he had seen as hairline and Hayley as canyon-like crevices.

He'd eventually returned home without a wife. And given no explanations for her absence other than she had left him. And that he didn't particularly care. He'd hidden his heartbreak behind that mask of indifference.

'Now I'm wishing I'd never come here,' Hayley said. 'How can I face her?'

'Does it matter?' he replied. 'You won't have to see my grandmother again after today. Or me. But for now, let's present a united front. To keep the peace for Dell and Alex's sake.'

'I'll try,' she said, slowly. 'They're really nice people.' To his relief, she stayed by his side.

Hayley braced herself. The last thing she wanted to do was cause a scene with Cristos's grandmother. But she wasn't twenty-two any more. Twenty-two and desperate to impress her new husband's family. Back then she might as well have festooned herself with signs begging them to like her. Now she had learned not to take rubbish from anyone, no matter their age. She had wanted approval and acceptance from Penelope, instead she had been crushed by rejection for no real reason that she could see.

Cristos's grandmother's shrewd black eyes flitted from Hayley to her grandson and back again. In spite of her resolve to stand up for herself, Hayley couldn't help but feel intimidated by the elderly Greek matriarch in full sail. She took a deep breath.

'It's always a surprise to see you, Hayley,' Penelope said in her charmingly accented English, with a smile that didn't reach those eyes. The surprise of their marriage had not been welcomed by Cristos's clan. Her surprise visit this time obviously wasn't either.

Before she could think of a suitable reply, Cristos spoke. 'A wonderful surprise, *Yia-yia*, that Hayley could join us for Alex and Dell's celebration.'

'Is that why you came here?' Penelope addressed her question to Hayley.

Hayley wasn't good at lying; she had to think about her reply. 'A loving marriage is an excellent thing to celebrate,' she said.

The old lady's eyes narrowed until they were mere slits in the wrinkles of her face. 'And your own marriage? Have you come back to be with your husband?'

'That's between Cristos and me,' Hayley said without hesitation.

'Hayley is right, *Yia-yia*.' Cristos's tone was kind—she knew how much he loved and respected his grandmother—but firm. His grip around Hayley's shoulder tightened and she automatically leaned in closer to him. Accepting his protection was something she had always done. Until she'd had to deal with the biggest crisis of her life without him.

Again Penelope addressed Hayley. 'You've put my grandson through hell, young lady. And if you—'

'There are always two sides to the story,' Hayley retorted. 'I—'

'Our seeing each other again really is our business,' said Cristos smoothly. 'While we appreciate your concern, you need to let us handle it in our own way.' He turned to Hayley. 'Isn't that right?'

Hayley nodded. 'It most certainly is.'

Penelope muttered something in Greek under her breath. Hayley had made an effort to learn Greek when she'd fallen in love with Cristos. She'd let it lapse with the end of their marriage; she didn't have the heart to speak Greek if it wasn't to her husband. But she knew enough to know that whatever Penelope had said wasn't polite. Hayley gritted her teeth. She did not want to get into an argument with Cristos's formidable grandmother. What would be the point? Their paths would not cross again after today. She looked up to him in mute appeal.

In response, Cristos looked deep into her eyes and smoothed the flyaway hair from her forehead with gentle fingers. Her breath caught at his touch, so familiar and yet so startlingly new, and she could not break her gaze from the deep green of his. 'I am so happy to have my wife back with me,' he murmured in that deep, rich, lightly accented voice that had always thrilled her.

Hayley knew he didn't mean that. It was a message for his grandmother—a subtle way of defusing the situation. But it felt anything but subtle to her as shivers of awareness rippled through her. Her body had not forgotten the pleasure his touch could bring.

It had been so long.

She lifted her face and closed her eyes to better savour the sensation as he made the act of smoothing her hair into a caress. She was so lost in the feeling she was totally unprepared when he kissed her.

Oh!

His mouth firm and warm on hers, the roughness of his chin, his scent, spicy and male. Her own lips soft and yielding under his. His hands sliding around her waist, pulling her closer. This felt so good. *Too good.* Her eyes flew open.

She didn't want this. Not this languorous warmth overtaking her. Not this feeling of being lost in his possession. Not this surge of awakening when she'd worked so hard to suppress her longing for him. She didn't want *him.* The marriage had been all on his terms—and in loving him so desperately she had lost herself.

She tried to pull away. 'We have to make this look believable,' he murmured against her mouth.

Why? She had agreed to play along with the charade of reconciliation so as not to disrupt his cousin's festivities. *Not* to kiss Cristos. She did not welcome the whoosh of long-banked-down embers igniting into flames. Because of a kiss. A simple—you could almost call it chaste—kiss.

'Don't kiss me again,' she murmured back against his mouth. His grandmother, watching intently, might take it for sweet talk. She stepped back with a shaky little laugh that sounded fake to her own ears but might fool the grandmother. The smile he gave her in return seemed equally fake, though ragged at the edges. And as soon as his grandmother headed away from them she shrugged herself free, making a play of smoothing down her coat.

'We should follow the others to lunch,' she said.

CHAPTER THREE

HAYLEY FOLLOWED CRISTOS into the dining area of the resort where some forty guests were gathering for an early lunch. In spite of all her resolve, she could not help but admire the splendour of the view of his back. His immaculately cut dark charcoal jacket—no doubt from the collection of his favourite Italian designer—worn with equally well tailored tapered trousers. The suit emphasised his broad shoulders and perfect behind, his long, leanly muscled legs. Cristos wore his clothes with effortless, masculine grace. No wonder he'd been such an instant hit as an international model.

Did he sense her gaze on him? He paused, turned back to her and reached out his hand. His eyes urged her to take it, for appearances' sake.

Her first instinct was to pull back from any further physical contact, even such a simple act as holding hands. It aroused too many memories of happier times. Times when she'd felt a surge of joy as Cristos's much larger hand had closed over hers. She had felt safe, protected and proud to let the world know that the extraordinarily handsome man by her side was hers. Then there were the memories of those skilful, loving hands on her body…

She shook her head to rid herself of unwanted thoughts. She especially didn't want to think about how she had reacted to his kiss back there in front of his grandmother. Those feelings should be firmly relegated to the past. She could not lose control of her life again. Since she had left him she had learned to be *herself* instead of the support act to her handsome, glamorous husband. She wanted it to stay that way.

But some kind of show of togetherness would be expected of a husband and wife having a civilised meeting and she didn't want to draw unwanted whispers from the people she knew were observing them. So she let her hand stay in his and made appropriate small talk about the resort as she walked by his side. It was just an act, she told herself, on his part as well as hers. He'd made steps towards divorce too. She could endure it for a few hours.

'You're not seeing the island at its best,' he said in a casual, conversational tone that anyone could overhear and think nothing of. She was grateful to him for that; she was aware that many ears in the room were tuned into their conversation hoping for a hint of what was going on between Cristos and the wife who had left him. Even if they could lip-read they wouldn't catch anything titillating. 'We're having an unusually cold winter,' he added.

The weather was always a useful standby but in this case it was a topic of genuine interest. The breeze that had outside played havoc with her hair had turned into something much stronger, buffeting the windows that looked out to the sea. The view was magnificent, the deep turquoise sea whipped up to whitecaps, grey clouds scudding across the sky.

'It must be breathtaking here in summer,' she said. 'But I can see the place has its own wild winter beauty too.'

'Kosmimo is special at any time of the year,' he said with an air of possession that surprised her. As far as she knew, his cousin Alex owned the island. But then his family were very close—

perhaps what belonged to one belonged to the others. Who knew? She had an older sister but they weren't particularly close.

Hayley didn't have to fake how impressed she was by her surroundings. The resort building was white and elegant in its simplicity as it stepped down the side of the slope to the sea and the single jetty that served the private island. As she had approached it by boat earlier in the day she had admired the way the structure sat so perfectly in the landscape.

The interiors exceeded all expectations—strikingly stylish with pale marble floors, white-washed woodwork, large shuttered windows and wide balconies facing the incredible view of the sea to the front and the forested hills to the back. It seemed serene, she thought, but with a subtle air of energy as well, fitting for a holistic resort where the guests came to rest and recharge. She was not surprised when Cristos told her the fit out had won design awards.

'Why is the resort called Pevezzo Athina?' she asked Cristos as he led her to their table.

'*Pevezzo* in the local dialect means safe haven. Athina is after our family-run *taverna* on the island of Prasinos not far from here. It's also the name of the restaurant my great-uncle, Alex's grandfather, started in Sydney.'

'So the name is a tradition,' she said. Once she had realised the connection to his family, she had not gone anywhere near that Sydney restaurant.

He nodded. 'Tradition is important to my family.'

When she had met him in Durham they had both been strangers away from home. His English had been near perfect, just slight differences in inflexion giving away that he was not a native speaker. They had been lovers and partners and husband and wife. The fact he was Greek and she was English hadn't mattered. It wasn't until they had visited Greece on their honeymoon that she had appreciated how Greek he was and how important his culture and traditions were to him.

'A safe haven.' She nodded slowly as she looked around her. 'I can see that. And the way the wind is starting to lash around the windows I want to feel safe.' She glanced down at her watch. 'Do you think it will be okay for you to take me back to Nidri in your boat after lunch?'

Cristos had suggested she cancel the return trip

she had booked with the boatman and let him take her back along with other guests in his bigger boat. Looking through the windows at how angry the sea had turned, she thought it had been a wise decision for her to agree.

He followed her gaze and frowned. 'We checked all the weather forecasts for this day when we were planning the celebration, but they didn't predict this. Hopefully it will blow over. Most of the guests need to leave after lunch. I'll check the reports again.'

From the time she had met him until the time she had left him, Hayley had leaned on Cristos. It was something she was determined never to do again. But checking weather forecasts in Greek was something she was happy to leave to him.

She knew she was gawking as she looked around her. The place really was extraordinary and she wasn't used to such high-end luxury. She earned a reasonable salary as a mechanical engineer, but a resort like this would be way out of her reach, the stuff of dream vacations. Cristos had coerced her into staying for lunch—she was determined to lap up the luxury and enjoy it.

True to her word, Dell had seated her at the

round table where she was already waiting with Alex. Hayley returned Dell's big smile. Dell was one of those people she had liked on sight. Under different circumstances she felt they would be friends.

'Kalos eerthes,' Dell said to her and Cristos. 'Welcome.' She introduced Hayley to the other guests at the table: cousins from Athens and two sets of parents, Dell's and Alex's, who had flown from Australia. The family connections were all too much for Hayley to take in, though she recognised some of the names from long-ago conversations with Cristos.

She was seated next to Cristos as was her due as his legally wed wife. It was surreal to be treated again as a couple, to be swept back into something that was once so everyday. *Hayley and Cristos.* They'd once been an entity. How much did his cousin and his wife know of their history? Hayley certainly didn't intend to mention anything of their future. The divorce was hers and Cristos's business alone.

However, she suspected Dell and Alex might have guessed not all was what it seemed between her and Cristos, the way they steered the conversation strictly to neutral territory. Alex explained the history of the island, how it had long ago been owned by Cristos's and Alex's family, more recently by a Greek magnate, then the Russian billionaire who had sold it back to Alex. He and Dell had developed the resort, building around an existing unfinished building.

Then there was chit-chat about the food. The meal was certainly conversation worthy. *Mezze* platters with a selection of Greek appetisers to start, followed by lamb and chicken cooked with lemon and Greek herbs, accompanied by seasonal vegetable dishes made with artichokes, beets and spinach.

'Most of what we're eating is grown on the island,' Cristos explained. 'Even the olive oil and the honey. The cheeses come from the milk from their herd of goats, and eggs from the chickens kept here.'

Hayley was surprised at his depth of knowledge about the resort and the island. Perhaps he had been working here for his cousin. As far as she knew he had stopped the lucrative modelling. She wondered what he had been doing since to earn a living. Her lawyer wanted to find out but

Hayley had instructed him that there was no need to investigate Cristos's finances. She didn't want to make any financial claim on him. A complete severing of ties was all that was required.

'It's fantastic to be practically self-sufficient for food,' she said. 'I saw water tanks and solar panels too.'

'The island is self-sufficient for power,' he said. 'I'm not surprised you noticed. You were always interested in alternative energy sources.'

'I'm working for a solar-panel development company in Sydney,' she said, then immediately regretted letting slip the information. Her life in Sydney was hers; her independence had been hard won. She didn't want to share the details of her new life with Cristos. When she went back she wanted to forget she had ever been married.

'Lots of sunshine in Australia, I guess,' was all he said. His eyes narrowed. She was grateful for the semi-public forum they found themselves in so he didn't press for details. Or perhaps he simply didn't care what she'd been doing with her life since she'd left him.

The placement of the chairs around the table was close—perhaps because they'd had to accommodate her as an extra guest. But it meant she was sitting very close to Cristos. Too close. Whatever she did—reach for condiments, lean aside to give access to the waiters—meant her shoulder brushed against his arm, his thigh nudged hers. She was as aware of the slightest contact as if there were a jolt of current connecting them. But it would appear too obvious to jump back from the contact.

She found the proximity disconcerting. Cristos seemed to take it in his stride. In front of a table of people he knew well, he played the role of husband with aplomb, always taking pains to include her in the conversation. Perhaps more so because he must be aware the other guests were dying to know the truth about the sudden reappearance of his English wife.

But this whole fake reunion thing was messing with her head. Particularly disconcerting had been her reaction to his kiss back at the chapel. She couldn't stop thinking about it. How could she have reacted like that when she was so determined to put him in her past?

The physical attraction between them when they'd met had been instant and magnetic. In the first blissful months of their marriage they had not been able to get enough of each other. Even when things had started to sour as he'd gone from business student to the hot man of the moment, any argument had ended up in bed. But physical attraction was not enough. Great sex was not enough.

She'd been so naïve when she'd met him. Maybe she'd been not just old-fashioned but misguided to insist on staying a virgin until marriage. Then she might not have rushed into marriage. That overwhelming hunger for him had blinded her to other issues that had in the end unravelled. Like trust. And honesty.

Right now she had to be honest with herself—she needed to fight that physical attraction so she could free herself from him and move on. Sitting so close to him at the table for lunch, she was preternaturally aware of him—every nuance in his expression, every shift in his body. He had once been her world.

It wasn't just his extraordinary good looks that were so compelling. It was also his effortless personal charisma. Switching between Greek and English, he had the entire table laughing at his story about a fishing expedition gone wrong. Yet when he turned to her, to translate a Greek phrase, his green eyes bright with laughter, it was as if she were the only person in the room who was of any importance to him. Once she had believed that to be true—before she'd had to share him with the rest of the world.

She forced a smile in response. He would know she was faking it but she hoped the others wouldn't. This was Dell and Alex's day and not to be marred by any antagonism between her and Cristos.

After the main course had been served, the guests on either side of both her and Cristos excused themselves from the table; those opposite were engrossed in conversation. Cristos picked up her left hand. 'You still wear your wedding and engagement rings,' he said in a low voice meant only for her.

'Just to transport them safely back to you,' she said. 'They're safer on my finger than in my handbag. I'll give them back to you when we say goodbye.'

His face tightened, all traces of his earlier good

humour extinguished. He released her hand. 'There is no need for that. The rings are yours.'

'What use are they to me?' she said. 'I'll never wear them again. And I don't want to be reminded of our marriage. I want to put all that behind me.' She had been in the nebulous state of being separated for too long. Not a wife, yet not single either.

He swore in Greek under his breath. Hurt? Pain? Anger? It certainly didn't sound like relief. She had agreed with Cristos not to disrupt the wedding renewal celebration. Now that she'd got to know Dell and Alex a little better she was glad she had stayed. But at what cost to her? And perhaps also to Cristos? She should never have come here.

'Did you wear your rings in Australia?' he asked abruptly.

She glanced down at the simple sapphire and diamond cluster set in white gold, the matching plain band. The stones in the engagement ring were tiny. When they'd got engaged Cristos couldn't afford anything more than a ring from a chain of high-street jewellers. But she'd thought it was beautiful and Cristos had declared the stone was nowhere nearly as beautiful as the colour of her eyes. Later, when the money from his new career had started to flow, he'd wanted to buy her a more expensive ring but she'd refused. She'd cherished that ring. It had symbolised everything good about their love. If he wouldn't take it back she would give it away.

'No. I didn't wear my rings in Sydney. And I didn't go by my married name either. I used my maiden name, Hayley Clements. It was easier than explaining a Greek surname when I so obviously didn't look Greek.'

Cristos slammed his right hand, where he wore his simple gold wedding band in the Greek tradition, on the table. 'I have never taken mine off,' he said.

Hayley swallowed the sudden lump in her throat. 'You took it off many times for your modelling shoots.'

'I was playing a role when I was working. Most often that role was not of a married man. I could not be seen to be wearing a wedding ring.'

'I understood that. Of course I did. But then you started to leave it off all the time.'

'You know why,' he said, tight-lipped. He shifted in his seat. This wedding-ring thing had become an issue in their short marriage. One that had festered with her in their time apart.

'Because it was seen as a disadvantage to your career to be married. A wife was a hindrance. *"It would be better for your fans—both female and male—if you were seen to be single."* Don't you remember your agent saying that?' She hadn't meant to blurt that out. She'd been determined not to speak of their mutual past. No recriminations. No blame. Just a clean cut.

He frowned. 'Of course I remember. We discussed it at the time—over and over. Then we agreed to take my agent's advice. We needed the money too much to argue with him.'

She looked down at the table. Smoothed a barely visible crease in the white tablecloth. When she'd got engaged to Cristos her parents had cut off her allowance, stopped the rent on her accommodation. They'd both been students. To get extra money, he'd tutored kids studying Greek, she'd taught dancing. Neither pursuit had been lucrative. They'd struggled.

'The idea was that we would still be together but not acknowledged as husband and wife,' she said. That still stung—though it had made sense at the time and she'd gone into it with eyes well and truly open. 'A girlfriend was acceptable. She was dispensable. That gave your fans hope that one day in their fantasies they might win you. The presence of a real-life wife ruined the fantasy.'

'That's how it was supposed to work,' he said. 'We both agreed I would take my wedding band off when I was in public. Then put it back on in private when I came home to you.'

Hayley couldn't keep the sadness from her voice as she looked back up at him. 'Until there were more and more times when you didn't come home. When you were on shoots all over Europe. Then exotic, far-flung places like Morocco and Africa.'

'Those jobs were the most lucrative,' he said, his jaw set. 'And the conditions weren't as glamorous as they looked. You didn't complain about the income they generated. I only did it for the money.'

Perhaps. But she would see the results of those shoots plastered all over billboards and in glossy magazines. More often than not they would feature Cristos, his body toned and buffed to perfection, wearing nothing more than swim-briefs or even underpants, with a gorgeous female model with next to nothing on draped all over him. She doubted even the most secure of wives wouldn't help but feel threatened. And a wife who had to keep her presence hidden, who didn't live up to the glamorous standards set by his new world, had found it difficult to deal with.

'You know I asked could you come with me,' he said. 'Repeatedly. It just wasn't done.'

The conversation was heading into territory Hayley had no wish to revisit. She picked up the little marble dish containing organic salt crystals from her place setting then put it down again. 'I know you tried to include me. And I appreciated it.'

On one stomach-churning occasion she had overheard his agent's reply when Cristos had asked could his beautiful wife perhaps join his agency as a model too. The agent had replied very quickly that it wasn't a good idea. *She's pretty enough. But she's too short and too wide in the hips.'*

His words had been so brutally dismissive. Even the word *pretty* had sounded like an insult. Was it then that she'd begun to believe that her husband's new world would not have room for her?

Cristos realised there were several ways Hayley looked different from when they'd been husband and wife. The short hair for one. But it was in her eyes he saw a shadow of sadness that wrenched at him.

'You're thinking about that comment my agent made, aren't you?'

Back then he had been furious at the insult to his wife and had wanted to walk out. He had cursed. He had fisted his hands by his sides to stop himself from punching the agent out.

But Hayley had swallowed the insult, had placated him and talked him into staying—for the sake of the money modelling had brought them. 'It's such an opportunity for us. How many people our age get that chance?' she'd said. Her strategy had been to put everything they saved into the bank to give them a better start than many young couples starting off life together. He'd preferred a riskier, higher-yielding investment option—but he hadn't told her that. Not then. Not ever.

Now she waved his comment away with a flick

of her wrist. 'I can laugh at that awful guy now,' she said. Cristos doubted that was true. 'I got used to people like him treating others like commodities, where the length of a woman's legs or the shape of a man's nose made them marketable or not.'

'Yeah. It could be brutal,' he said. In Cristos's eyes, Hayley had been the most beautiful woman in the world. His agent had seen her differently. If a woman wasn't fit for purpose then she had no use. Or a man. That was an inescapable reality of the business. And one he'd ultimately walked away from. He'd only endured it for her sake. When they'd discovered she was pregnant he had worked even longer hours for financial security for his wife and child.

It wasn't a business Cristos had signed up for intentionally. Six months after they'd married, when he had finished his master's degree in business and Hayley still had a term to go to finish her degree in engineering, they'd taken the train down to London for a mini-break.

Cristos's patience for shopping was limited. While Hayley had looked through every dress on the rack in a boutique in Covent Garden, Cristos had leaned against a wall outside and waited for her. Hands shoved deep into the pockets of his black jacket, he'd been happy to watch the world go by. London and the people from all around the world who flocked to it had fascinated him.

When the very fashionably dressed middle-aged man had approached him and asked him had he ever considered being a model, he'd brushed him off. Less politely the second time. Cristos had never lacked female attention, and often male attention too. He hadn't wanted to insult the guy but he'd made it clear in no uncertain terms that whatever pick-up line the older man chose to use it would not work on him. He was a happily married man.

Cristos had taken the man's card just to get him off his back. It had indeed been from a talent agency but anyone could print off a business card and make it say whatever they wanted. He'd put it in his pocket and forgotten about it.

Later at lunch in an Italian restaurant off Leicester Square he'd remembered and pulled the card out of his pocket to show Hayley. Her eyes had widened. 'If that guy was genuine, this is one of the biggest model agencies in the world. I think you should follow it up.'

'Me? A model?' he'd scoffed. He'd thought himself way too macho to even consider it. In his world, modelling wasn't a serious man's profession. 'No way. Never.'

'You're more than good-looking enough,' Hayley had said, her eyes narrowed thoughtfully. 'Ask them what kind of money you could make.'

The model scout had, in fact, been genuine. And the potential earnings Cristos had been quoted had been enough for him and Hayley to turn to each other and grin. When the agent had moved away to a filing cabinet to get a contract, they'd given each other a high five behind his back. 'This might be fun,' she'd said, laughing.

Turned out Cristos had had just the look big-brand clients wanted. In a sea of underfed, androgynous male models he'd stood out with his muscular build and intense masculinity. He'd been booked solid straight away. Had been hailed almost immediately as the new David Gandy.

But commuting from Durham in the north of England had become problematic. He'd moved to a small flat in Camberwell in South East London and seen Hayley as often as they had been able to manage between her studies and his modelling commitments. It hadn't worked. They hadn't been able to bear to spend so much time apart. He had missed her with an intensity that had made it difficult to concentrate on his work. She'd deferred her final term and moved to London to be with him. Stints in Paris and Milan had followed. And Hayley had never got the chance to go back to university.

'Are you still modelling?' Hayley asked.

He shook his head. 'After you left, I honoured existing contracts then retired.'

'And came home to Greece?' She paused. 'You don't have to answer that question. What you do now is none of my business.'

He wanted to say that of course his life was her business. Legally she was still his wife. But that would involve coming clean about his taking risks with their savings—even though it had paid off more than handsomely. He hadn't felt able to tell her then. Nor to mention that one of his collaborators had been female. For such a sweet, petite woman Hayley could be very feisty and he hadn't wanted to face her justifiable wrath. By the time he'd hit the jackpot with that first online shopping comparison app, she'd been gone from his life.

Now it would all come out in the property settlement. No doubt her lawyers had burrowed into his business and discovered his net worth down to the last cent. This divorce wouldn't come cheap. Perhaps that was why she'd come here—time for her to collect financially from their brief marriage. Whatever she was legally due, she would get. But no more. He would not fund her life with a new man.

She was playing her part well but he noticed her getting edgy about leaving—this time for ever. She tried to be discreet about checking her watch but he noticed. Dessert would be served soon. When that was over, he would have no choice but to take her off the island in his boat. He had to manoeuvre some private time with her. Otherwise he might never get answers to his question.

'Hayley, I want to—'

But he got no further.

'Cristos. I need to talk to you.' Alex's voice was low and urgent. Startled, Cristos looked up to find his cousin standing behind him. He'd been so intent on his conversation with Hayley he hadn't noticed that Alex had left the table.

His grandfather Stavros was also there. Both wore grave expressions. 'There's a weather alert,' said Alex. 'A severe storm approaching. Big seas. No boats can leave the island.'

There was a gasp from Hayley beside him. 'You mean we're stuck here? But I need to—'

Cristos sensed the panic in her words. Stuck on the island meant stuck with *him*. The man she had come here to divorce.

Alex completely misunderstood Hayley's panic. 'Don't worry, Hayley. We'll be safe here,' he reassured her. 'There's room for all the guests to stay overnight. The storm will most likely blow over by the morning. I'll put you and Cristos in the penthouse. It's the best room in the house and only fitting for you to celebrate your reunion.'

'The penthouse?' she said, barely able to get the words out. 'Isn't that reserved for you and Dell?'

Alex dismissed her objection with a wave of his hand. 'We have our own house on the island.'

He looked pleased with himself for giving them the penthouse and the privacy he seemed to assume they needed to rekindle their relationship.

Hayley's face had drained of all colour.

Cristos fought to supress a grin of exultation at this unexpected new hand he'd been dealt.

He would be spending more time with his wife.

CHAPTER FOUR

HAYLEY COULD NOT, *would* not, share a room with Cristos. 'No way. Never. Not in a million years,' she hissed at him after Alex had left them. She stood braced with her back to the table. 'I can't stay here. Isn't there another way to get off this island?'

'No,' he said.

Panic strangled her lungs so her breath came short, set her heart pounding. Why, why, why had she done the right thing by Cristos's cousin and ended up like this? She should be back on Nidri and on the way back to Sydney. Everything had seemed so simple as she'd geared herself up for it on the flight from London where she'd met with her lawyer—deliver the divorce documents, have polite exchange with love of her youth, move on to new life and forget he had ever happened. She hadn't counted on that intense flare of the old attraction. Now *this*.

She managed a deep breath to calm herself. 'That can't be true. I saw a helipad behind the main building.'

'Wealthy guests use it in summer. There's no helicopter here now and even if there was it wouldn't be safe to fly. It's hazardous conditions for boats and aircraft. There is no way off or on the island.' His tone left no room for uncertainty.

Hayley's eyes narrowed. 'Did you plan this?' she said, keeping her voice low. 'Did you know when you coerced me into staying for the lunch that this would happen? That I'd be stuck here unable to get away?'

Cristos stared at her. 'Why would you say that? Choppy seas were predicted but not a storm of this magnitude. My family have been sailing these seas for ever, *koukla*, we know—'

'Don't call me *koukla*,' she interjected.

'Force of habit,' he said.

He rolled his eyes, which rather than making her indignant made her, in her semi-hysterical state, want to smile. She clamped her lips together to fight it. That was the trouble with Cristos. He could charm you even when you didn't want to be charmed. She could not let herself be ensnared by that charm again.

Cristos continued. 'From the reports we saw this morning I was totally confident I would be taking guests off the island this afternoon. Even the weather forecasters have been caught out by this storm. The weather has been so unpredict-able. This is the coldest winter for many years.'

Her eyes narrowed. 'Are you sure you didn't suspect this storm might happen earlier, when it would still have been safe for me to leave? That you kept me here knowing this might happen?'

'I swear not.' He frowned. 'When did I ever force you into doing something you didn't want to do?'

She looked up at him and was struck by the sincerity in his eyes. Those remarkable eyes that she had seen sparked by love and desire and righ-teous anger but never force. He had wheedled her and teased her and kissed her into agreeing with him but he had never forced her to do anything against her will.

'Never,' she said. She had willingly let herself be carried along by the force of his personality because nothing had been more important to her than being with him.

'I don't fly out of the airport at Preveza until tomorrow so staying here tonight won't be a total disaster. That being so, I still don't want to share a room with you. I have to have a room by myself.'

'Not possible,' he said. 'As it is, people will have to double up in rooms. It's a privilege for us to be given the penthouse just to ourselves.'

She closed her eyes. This must be some kind of nightmare. But when she opened her eyes he was still there. All six feet two of handsome soon-to-be-ex-husband she so desperately didn't want to be near. *Trapped.* 'I could share a room with someone else.'

His dark brows rose in an infuriating manner. 'Really? Who?'

She cast a quick glance towards the other tables. She didn't know another soul well enough to share a room with them. Certainly not Grandma Penelope.

She made a sweep of her arm around the airy white room. 'I could sleep down here somewhere.'

'And freeze? The temperature will plummet overnight.'

'Maybe you could—'

'Forget it. I'm not sleeping down here either. Not only is it too cold it would have everyone talking about us. We're still married. People don't know it's not for much longer. It's expected we would share a room.'

He stepped closer. Put both hands on her shoulders. To anyone watching it would seem like an affectionate gesture. He spoke in a low, urgent undertone. 'Please don't kick up a fuss. The other guests are in the same situation. This is not what Alex and Dell need. It could ruin their day completely if everyone started complaining that they needed a single room.'

'But all the other guests wanted to be on the island. I'm here by default. I really can't be here with—'

'With me. You've made that clear,' he said. 'You don't need to be frightened of me, Hayley.'

'Frightened?' Her chin rose. 'Of course I'm not.'

Didn't he realise? She wasn't frightened of *him*. She was frightened of herself. The more time she spent with him, the more she feared her attraction to him. The more she risked leaving this island with her heart torn and aching over what could no longer be with the man she had married with such high hopes.

'It's inconvenient, I know. But like everyone else here you have to accept it.' He shrugged broad shoulders. 'Why not think of it as an adventure? When we…'

'When we what?' She had a horrible feeling he was laughing at her. That he liked seeing her put on the spot. Payback for the way she'd left him.

'When we were first together we would have thought being forced to stay the night in a luxury hotel for free would have been an adventure.'

Of course, it would have. They would have ordered room service, would never have got out of bed. They would have made love in the bathtub… *Stop.* That was yesterday. A different life. A different relationship. A different Cristos.

'Yes,' she said, knowing everything she was thinking must be showing in her eyes and seeing the same thoughts reflected in his. Their gaze held for a long time until she looked away.

A spasm of that old longing shuddered through her. In that lay danger. She remembered those long lonely nights when he was away from her, where her imagination had tortured her with thoughts of what he could be doing with the beautiful female models who worked with him. Then the night she had lost the baby when she'd needed him so desperately and he hadn't responded to her calls. The more she'd loved him, the more she'd ached for him every minute they'd been apart. Then the worse she'd felt when all those dreams and hopes they'd held in trust had shattered.

'I remember those times only too well,' she said. 'Which is why I'm seriously considering taking the risk of catching pneumonia and sleeping down here tonight.'

He sighed. The *you are testing my patience* sigh she also remembered. 'No need for that. The penthouse has a king-sized bed and a sofa. I'll take the sofa,' he said.

Even having him in the same room would be distraction enough. There would be no chance of sleep. But it seemed she had no choice. 'Okay,' she said reluctantly. 'If we can just stay out of each other's way it might be all right. After all, it's only for one night.'

Behind Cristos's mask of relaxed indifference simmered a heady elation. *One night.* He had one night with Hayley where she would, indeed, be trapped with him. Not trapped in any malevolent sense. Rather she would be forced into his company in the close proximity of a private hotel room.

Alone with Hayley for the first time in two and a half years. And despite her determination to divorce, he had twice glimpsed a hint of something very like desire in her eyes. Maybe he had wanted to see her answering desire so badly he had imagined it, maybe he hadn't. But a gambler got used to reading body language—and he had known her as intimately as only a loving husband could.

There was that simple kiss staged for his grandmother's benefit. Just a brief kiss. Yet it had ignited an old hunger in him. He had convinced himself it was extinguished, that it had gone to ashes. But the embers had been there, had burst into flames at the touch of her lips. By the way she'd reacted, it seemed she had felt it too.

He had wanted her from the get-go—and she'd felt the same. She'd been an innocent when they'd first met, determined, in spite of the sensual hunger he'd aroused in her with his kisses, to preserve her virginity until her wedding night. She'd had her reasons and he had respected her choice, admired it even. In his traditional culture a virgin wife was prized, although he certainly hadn't expected her to be chaste. Once they were married he'd been surprised and delighted at her passion and enthusiasm for lovemaking. No matter what else might have gone wrong in their relationship, they had been utterly in tune in bed.

Now he would be once more sharing a bedroom with her. But he had meant it when he'd said he'd sleep on the sofa. A fling with his soon-to-be-ex-wife wasn't on the cards. Even if she were willing, which seemed highly unlikely. Not when she backed away from even holding hands with him.

He would grab this chance to ask questions. No doubt she had questions of her own. They needed to talk. Something, he had come to realise in the soul-searching time they'd been apart, he should have done more of when they were together. Instead of silencing her concerns about the turn their life together had taken with kisses, he should have listened to her.

While legally Hayley was still his wife, he knew he had lost her nearly two and a half years ago. This night together was a gift and he had to be careful not to squander it. He had to get answers to his questions. Why had she pushed him away from her that night when she'd lost the baby instead of grieving together? Why had she run so far away? What had she been doing in Australia? Who was this other guy and did he pose a threat?

Was there any hope of a second chance with the woman he had never stopped wanting?

But right now she had questions of her own. Practical questions as befitted his down-to-earth, organised wife. Soon-to-be-ex-wife unless things between them changed dramatically, he had to remind himself.

Hayley tapped her booted foot with such annoyance he had to suppress a smile. That short haircut made her look like a cranky pixie. 'How can this work? My suitcase is in a hotel in Nidri. I don't have a change of clothes. Scarcely any cosmetics. All I have is a toothbrush and paste from the plane in my handbag.'

'You don't need cosmetics,' he said. 'You're beautiful without them.' He didn't mean that to sound cheesy. The compliment had come automatically.

She flushed high on her cheekbones. 'So you always said.'

'But you never believed me.'

'It was difficult when you worked with those gorgeous models.'

'Some of whom were so plain without make-up you wouldn't give them a second look.'

'But the camera loved them, you said.'

'Whereas you look lovely with or without make-up,' he said. 'A natural beauty.'

'Pretty, remember, not beautiful,' she said with a downturned twist to her mouth. 'Not that I care about the difference.'

He added another curse to the number he had already hurled at his then agent for the thoughtless comment that had so wounded Hayley. Seemed that wound still hadn't healed.

'There is nothing wrong with pretty,' he said. 'In fact it's very, very right. You're looking good, Hayley. Life in Sydney must suit you.'

'I like it,' she said dismissively. No answers there, then. 'But talking about Sydney is not solving my problem now.'

'The resort store will stock everything you need.'

'Like pyjamas?'

Since when had she started wearing pyjamas? There'd been no need for pyjamas in their marriage.

'There are some very smart pyjamas there.' Dell had stocked the small store with the upscale resort-branded products wealthy customers did not hesitate to spend on. 'Dell has probably already thought to open the store. You won't be the only one who might need to stock up. Whatever you need I'll pay for, of course.'

Hayley drew herself up to her full diminutive height. 'That won't be necessary. I have some euros and my credit card with me.'

He shook his head. 'It's my fault you're stranded here. I insist on paying for whatever you need.'

Her chin lifted in the stubborn way he remembered only too well. 'In that case I won't get pyjamas. I'll go without.' She must have caught a gleam in his eyes at the thought of Hayley in bed with nothing covering her but the sheets because she faltered to a halt. 'I insist on paying my own way. Some Greek pyjamas might be a nice souvenir to take home with me to Sydney.'

He shrugged. 'Have it your way,' he said, pleased

that he could fluster her. He'd arrange with Dell for any payment on Hayley's card to be reversed so she wouldn't be out of pocket.

'What about you? You weren't expecting to stay the night either, were you?'

'You know I never wear pyjamas.' He watched, amused, as her blush deepened.

'Uh...yes. I remember.' She seemed to take a sudden interest in the marbling of the floor beneath them.

He let her off the hook. 'But in this case I will also ensure I wear something to bed. I keep some clothes in the office here.'

She looked up at him again. 'Do you spend much time here? You seem to take a great interest in the resort.'

He should tell her he was a co-owner, having invested in the resort at the start. But that would involve telling her so much more and now wasn't an appropriate time. No doubt her lawyer would discover what he owned. 'I work alongside Alex,' he said. 'It's somewhat of a family business.'

'As is your tradition.'

'That's right,' he said.

'I…well, I wondered. I have no idea what you've been doing in the years since I last saw you.'

Tonight, he would clearly not be the only one asking questions. He needed to think how he would answer her questions without revealing how much he had left unsaid during their marriage. His habit of masking his true self to the woman he'd loved had backfired. He had told himself he was working towards their future. But he couldn't deny that he had hidden from her the truth of what he was—a gambler and a risk taker, his father's son. No amount of subsequent safe investments that had secured his fortune could change that.

He had feared if she had known what he really was, she would have spurned him. From the start he'd known her middle-class parents had looked down on him. How could he have admitted that his father had been in prison—not once but multiple times? That would only have reinforced their opinion of him as an unsuitable spouse for their daughter. And perhaps made Hayley start to believe it.

'He's NQOC, dear,' he had overheard her mother say about him to Hayley the only time she had taken her new boyfriend home to her family's house in a gated estate in posh Surrey.

Cristos hadn't told Hayley what he'd heard, hadn't asked her what her mother had meant. But back in Durham he'd asked an English friend what it had meant. 'Not Quite Our Class,' his friend had explained, puzzled that anyone would use such an outdated and snobbish expression.

Cristos had been both horrified and furious that Hayley's mother had used such a term about *him*. He was proud of his hardworking and honest grandparents, his relatives who owned fishing boats and *tavernas*, no matter what 'class' Hayley's mother might assign them to.

But then there was the reality of his jailbird father. His grandparents could quite likely have given his *baba* the same snooty label. They had despised him and seen their daughter's husband as the biggest mistake of his mother's life. When Cristos had gone into their care, they had instilled in him that his father was someone to be ashamed of—so ashamed they would have liked to deny his existence.

Cristos had told Hayley his father had died but not the circumstances of his death. The odds against them as a young couple facing opposition to their marriage had been high enough without throwing that into the game. That and the underlying fear he had inherited his father's bad traits—although the years since had proved him to be a hard-working businessman.

There would be so much at stake tonight. Much as he might want to, he would not try and seduce Hayley into that king-sized bed in the penthouse. Because, before anything else, he had to win her trust. Without that he had no hope of discovering the truth and making reparation for their past.

As Alex went from table to table with the news about the storm, a babble of chatter erupted in the room.

'I don't think I'm the only one not happy about being stuck on the island,' Hayley said with a wry smile.

'It seems that way, doesn't it?' he said. 'Do you mind if I go and give Alex a hand?'

'Please do,' she said.

'Will you be all right by yourself?'

'Of course. I can see Dell's parents heading back towards the table. I'll have someone to talk to.'

'I'll get back to you as soon as I can.'

'Don't worry about me,' she said. 'I'm a big girl used to looking after myself now.'

And I don't need you were her unspoken words that came through to him loud and clear and as sharp as a shard of ice stabbing his heart.

She still had the power to hurt him.

CHAPTER FIVE

HAYLEY KNEW ONLY too well the look of another woman who desired her husband. One of the perils of being married to a man as handsome and charismatic as Cristos was that other women wanted him too. And were sometimes blatant about letting their interest be known.

After lunch, the guests had gathered in the resort's meditation room, a large, airy space overlooking the water. It was there she saw the open, hungry yearning on the face of a dark-haired, attractive Greek woman who stood opposite her, shoulder to shoulder with Cristos's grandmother.

Hayley had to look away, swallowing against a sudden surge of nausea. She'd thought she'd got immune to the kick-in-the-stomach feeling that kind of undisguised look caused her. Seemed not. Maybe she never would. It shouldn't matter now that she and Cristos were on the brink of divorce. Yet her heart still felt scorched.

In the first blissful months of their relationship, other women's reactions to her husband's extraordinary good looks had never bothered her. Secure in his love, she had laughed and said how lucky she was Cristos had chosen her. 'You'd better believe it, *koukla*,' he'd used to say.

But as his career had unexpectedly skyrocketed, so had the level of female interest. A mini-movie-type commercial for a luxury men's cologne had gone viral—shared all over the internet—delighting the advertiser and making a star out of Cristos. Neither she nor Cristos had anticipated the attention it would bring him. To give her husband his due, he had never encouraged his admirers. But Hayley hadn't realised that, by agreeing to be a secret wife, she would have to endure seeing other women openly lust after her husband.

And here she was facing it again. She had left Cristos nearly two and a half years ago. Her choice. She could not reasonably expect that he'd been on his own all that time. But the thought of him with someone else was still unbearable. Who was this woman? And why was Cristos so insistent on them presenting as a married couple if his girlfriend was around?

Hayley closed her eyes and wished she were anywhere else but the island of Kosmimo. She could do without this added angst. All she wanted was to be free of the soul-destroying insecurities that had come part and parcel with her marriage. And then to move on.

The meditation room was minimally furnished in shades of white to allow people to meditate or practise mindfulness without distraction. Silence was usually a requirement. It was anything but that now with the buzz of people concerned about the disruption to their travel plans. Alex and Dell's families from Australia had planned to stay on anyway so weren't complaining. But some of the guests were from Athens, others the surrounding islands. It was Saturday and they were concerned about getting back to work on Monday. Hayley hoped she'd be allowed to leave on the first boat in the morning to make her connections to first Athens, then Dubai, for her flight to Sydney.

Cristos took to the floor with Alex to explain how their enforced stay at Pevezzo Athina would be handled in terms of accommodation and meals. Dell stood by to hand out keys to the rooms they had allocated their unexpected overnight guests. Dell's children were in the care of their two sets of grandparents from Australia who seemed to compete with each other to be the most doting.

If only... What might it be like to be here with her own child toddling around with his or her little cousins? Part of a big, welcoming family? Hayley pushed the thought right to the shadowed back of her mind where painful memories had been relegated. Instead of being a beloved wife and mother she stood on the sidelines of Cristos's family, never welcomed into it, and now straining to break the legal bonds to it.

The dark-haired woman couldn't tear her gaze from Cristos's face as he effortlessly commanded the attention of everyone in the room. At one stage, Penelope leaned up to whisper something in the younger woman's ear, and then looked pointedly towards Hayley. What was that about? Hayley flushed. But she held the old woman's gaze and nodded in acknowledgment of the exchange. She refused to be cowed.

But when Cristos returned to Hayley's side, she didn't say anything about the woman or his grandmother's obvious attachment to her. Truth be told, she didn't really know what to say. No longer did she have the right to question him. And, perhaps, she wanted to spare herself his answers.

'That seemed to go well,' she said instead. 'Poor Dell and Alex having their day end like this. What rotten luck.'

'Or they could look at it that the party goes on for so much longer than intended,' Cristos said with a grin. 'The resort is well stocked with food and drink and all these people are their friends.'

'That's one way of looking at it,' she said, unable to resist an answering smile. But she was aware of the dark-haired woman's eyes drilling into her now and it made her self-conscious. She had to say something. She moved closer to Cristos, kept her voice low so her words were only for him. 'That woman standing next to your grandmother, the gorgeous dark-haired one. Is she... are you...?' Her throat closed around the words.

Cristos looked deep into her face, not taking his eyes from hers for even a second to look across to the woman. To anyone looking it would seem as if they were exchanging intimate talk. 'You mean Arianna? The answer is no and no.'

Hayley swallowed against an inexplicable relief. 'She's giving you "the look",' she said. She didn't need to explain any further. In those early days, when him being a successful male model was still fun, they'd laughed together about how predatory some of the women had been. Not to mention the men.

'She's being encouraged by my grandmother to do so,' he said with a low groan.

'While Penelope believes we're still married? I should be grossly offended by that.'

'I'm not defending my *yia-yia's* behaviour. But you were away a long time.' His mouth said one thing, his eyes so much more. Anger. Betrayal. Loss.

She gritted her teeth. Answered only his words. 'I know that. It's just disconcerting to have your grandmother encouraging my successor while I'm still here.'

His dark brows rose. 'Your successor? Arianna was here before I ever met you. I chose you over her long ago. In fact there was no choice to make. Her grandparents are friends with my grandparents. Penelope considers herself a *promnestria*, a matchmaker.'

'In our case she tried to be a match-breaker.'

'Maybe so,' he said. 'She had Arianna earmarked for me from when we were babies.'

'Oh.' Hayley was angry at herself for the hurt that crept into her voice. 'I can see why. She's beautiful. And sexy.'

Still Cristos didn't look over to Arianna. His eyes were only for her. He cupped her chin in his hand so she was forced not to evade his gaze. 'I dated her once when we were sixteen. It was a mistake. I wasn't interested in her then and I'm certainly not now. How could I be when you are here, *kou*—?' He stopped himself from completing the word.

He seemed determined to make this as difficult as he could for her, using his pet name for her, invoking the past. She did not want to remember such a deeply unhappy part of her life or to endure recriminations or blame. He had said he wanted the same thing she did—divorce. She screwed up her face in appeal. 'Cristos, please—'

He turned his head away so she could no longer see the unspoken message in his eyes. When he looked back to her his gaze showed only unconcerned good humour. 'Yes. I know you are only here to divorce me. But that doesn't stop me from thinking you're more beautiful than any other woman I know.'

He dropped a light kiss on her mouth. For Arianna's benefit? His grandmother's? Or to remind her of just what a kiss from him could do to her? If it was the latter, he succeeded as a thrill of delight tingled through her body. His kisses had delighted her from the very first time on the night they'd met.

She stepped back. Crossed her arms across her chest. 'Thank you,' she said, knowing it would be ungracious not to accept the compliment. And to block the traitorous racing of her heart. It was frightening how her body still reacted to his touch.

She couldn't face his gaze again. Who knew what she might see in those eyes this time? Instead she looked across through the floor-to-ceiling glass doors that led out onto a marble balcony. They were obviously designed to frame a view of sparkling sun-kissed aquamarine waters and blue skies. Ominous dark clouds were banking up out to sea, obliterating the sky, their shadows darkening the choppy sea below to a sullen grey. A sudden gust of wind made the glass shudder.

Cristos followed her gaze. 'You can see why we couldn't take a boat out in that. The storm is gathering strength. It's going to be fierce when it hits.'

'What are you doing to secure the building?' she asked.

'Alex and I will get some of the guys to go outside and make sure—'

'I'll come too,' she said.

'Perhaps you can help Dell inside,' he said, relegating her to the 'women's work' of the traditional Greek family.

She squared up to him. 'You might not know that I finished my degree in mechanical engineering at the University of New South Wales in Sydney. I'm working as an engineer and considered very competent. You must remember me telling you I worked as a teenager with my father on all the home maintenance. I probably know more about what to do than you or Alex.'

Cristos looked down at her with a mixture of admiration and reluctant defeat. 'You're probably right,' he said.

'Not that I'm taking anything away from your Greek male authority,' she said, teasing him the way she used to. Then realised she shouldn't say anything that could be construed as flirtatious.

'Of course not,' he said. 'I learned early on not to underestimate you.'

Then later on you took me for granted, she thought, but didn't say.

She glanced down at her expensive biscuit-coloured trousers and fine ivory cashmere sweater—both from her life with him after his meteoric success when designer clothes came easy. 'I'll go to the resort store and buy some jeans and a sweatshirt, see if Dell can loan me a weatherproof jacket.'

'If that's what you want to do.'

She felt trapped. Trapped on the island, trapped with him, held hostage by old emotions and hurts. She needed to do something. Not just stand around wringing her hands over her plight or using her enforced time as an excuse to party. She needed to roll up her sleeves and work. Doing something useful might take her mind off her body's reaction to his touch. Then there was the blatant interest of another woman in the man she had once thought she would grow old with. Too much of the past was coming back to haunt her and taunt her.

'I'll get a team together and meet you at the utility area,' Cristos said.

'Right,' she said.

He handed her a key card. 'It's to our room.'

Our room.

That was another disconcerting event she hoped a good dose of solid physical work—like shoring up windows and checking electrical connections—might take her mind off. The prospect of sharing a bedroom with the man who was still legally her husband.

Hayley's laughter pealed out from the direction of the pool house. High on a ladder, Cristos paused in his task of securing the upper-storey window shutters. He hadn't heard that joyous sound for too many years and he stilled when he realised how much he had missed it.

He turned and his eyes widened at the improbable sight of his wife—he couldn't think of her as anything other—working together with his grandfather. They were moving the outdoor furniture from around the swimming pool to where it would be safe in the case of high winds.

It wasn't a matter of Hayley assisting Stavros—young Englishwoman deferring to Greek patriarch. Rather his petite wife and his aged and somewhat stout grandfather were well matched in terms of strength and made a surprisingly effective team. They'd already cleared the gardens of any equipment that had been left lying around.

He was further surprised by the sound of his grandfather's gruff laughter. Stavros was a man of few words; he always said his wife, Penelope, had words enough for both of them. Since the death of his only daughter, he was also a man of little laughter.

What had Hayley said to provoke that rusty laughter from the man who had disapproved of his grandson's marriage to an English stranger every bit as vehemently as his wife had done? Cristos decided not to question it, but to enjoy it.

The cold wind whipping his face raw, he watched Hayley and Stavros for a long moment. He imagined an alternate universe in which he and Hayley were still married, living perhaps in London, and visiting the family in Greece for

Alex and Dell's vow-renewal ceremony. In this happy world, Hayley was a much-loved member of his extended family, Penelope extending to her the same warmth and welcome as she did to Dell. While he and Hayley worked outside to secure the resort against the coming storm, their child—he'd hoped for a boy but would have loved whatever baby they'd been gifted—was safely inside playing with Litza, her little cousin. At night he and Hayley would sink happily into bed, drowsing off to sleep in each other's arms after making love knowing they had tomorrow and all the tomorrows after it together.

That was where he had to put the brakes on his daydream. He stared at the window he was meant to be securing. In the reflection he saw his face looking tight and haggard, hardly the image of Europe's one-time top male model—the role he had come to hate. It had lost him everything he had valued. His wife. His unborn child. His future.

Hayley had never acknowledged his anguish and grief at the loss of the baby he had wanted so much. In fact she had pushed him away from her. Perhaps her own grief had been so intense she hadn't been able to deal with his. He didn't know. She hadn't given him the chance to comfort her—or she him.

He looked down again at Hayley and his grandfather, chatting companionably as, in the looming evening, they walked towards the pool house where both sets of visiting Australian parents, Alex's and Dell's, were staying. He couldn't hear what they were actually saying from this distance but their voices carried enough for him to realise Hayley was trying to speak Greek with Stavros and he was correcting her usage. Not in a disparaging way but in a helpful way, obviously pleased that she had tried to learn their language. Perhaps her mistakes had prompted the laughter.

A wave of overwhelming sadness swept over him, sending his determined optimism tumbling over and over as it struggled not to drown. Somehow he and Hayley had detoured from the path their marriage should have taken. He was not at all certain it was possible after all this time apart to right past wrongs and consider the possibility of getting it back on track. He doubted they could even salvage a friendship. Perhaps this gambler should accept it was time for him to throw in his cards.

For nearly two and a half years when people had asked him why his wife had left him he had shrugged and said, as if it didn't bother him, 'I don't know.' *He still didn't know.*

Then both his wife and his grandfather, sensing perhaps the intensity of his gaze on them, turned and saw him. In perfect synchronicity, they waved to him. With the hand that was not gripping the ladder, he waved to them in return, forcing a smile he hoped they could see.

At their answering smiles, the gloom receded. He had tonight with Hayley. Just him and her, with nowhere for her to run. He was determined to make the most of it. If there was ever to be a chance for them to understand what had gone wrong, this was it.

CHAPTER SIX

OUTSIDE, EVERYTHING AROUND Hayley had gone very still and the island seemed quiet with expectation. Nobody had asked her to look at the solar panels but she'd wanted to check them anyway. Air like icy needles stung her face and she shivered. The sky darkened with an ominous yellow tinge and she hastened to make it safely back inside the resort.

As she pulled off the work gloves Stavros had found for her and shrugged out of Dell's too-big jacket, Hayley looked around for Cristos. She'd lost track of him; last seen he'd been working alongside Alex fixing a loose shutter. She wrapped her arms around herself. It felt odd not to have him by her side. There was no role for her in this place without him.

What was she doing here?

The storm hit with its full fury just minutes later, in a frenzy of crashing thunder and lightning that forked through the sky. Violent winds whipped around the building. Rain lashed against the windows with the sound of pebbles being hurled against the glass. The building shuddered and shook with each assault from the skies.

The guests had all been allocated their rooms, but many now gathered again in the far from quiet meditation room. Hayley joined them; it was more comforting to be among people even though she was still the object of either curious glances or tentative smiles. She suspected, as far as support for Cristos's errant wife went, they might have divided into Team Penelope and Team Dell.

Alex reassured everyone in the room that the resort was well built and sturdy and they were all perfectly safe. But children among the guests screamed with each crash of thunder until their parents made a game of it that had the kids competing who could jump the highest when the thunder erupted.

Dell's toddler Litza joined in with the bigger kids, attempting to jump but not getting very high and then chortling with sweet baby peals of laughter. She was adorable but Hayley found it unbearable to watch her. Most of the time she didn't allow herself to wonder what her baby—girl or boy—would be like now if her pregnancy had proceeded. She had forced herself to bury such painful thoughts. But Litza, her baby words alternating between English and Greek as her child would likely have done, was too much of a reminder of what she'd lost, what might have been.

She turned her back on the kids and stood watching the sky, keeping a safe distance away from the glass doors in the meditation room. She would be out of here tomorrow and this would seem in retrospect like a bad dream.

Every so often lightning would illuminate the darkness, reflecting in the roiling sea below. She sensed Cristos come up behind her. After all this time, she still recognised his footfall, his scent, his presence, *him*.

'Here you are,' he said, as a husband seeking his wife might say. He took his place beside her, close enough that his arm brushed against her, showing—consciously or not—to anyone watching them that they were a couple. He didn't say anything else, rather joined her watching the pyrotechnics display in the sky for a surprisingly companionable moment.

'They say the negative ions released into the atmosphere by an electrical storm can make you feel wonderful,' she said, without turning to him. 'I wish I could go outside and breathe them in but I know it wouldn't be safe with all that lightning about.'

'Why is that? The ions, I mean.'

She slanted her shoulder towards him; in profile he looked pensive and heartbreakingly handsome. Was he really interested in ions or just asking so they would appear deep in husband-and-wife conversation?

'Apparently they cause some kind of biochemical reaction that releases feel-good hormones in the body.' She didn't mention that she'd read the effect of the negative ions included heightened sensual awareness—back when they were together it would have been the first thing she'd told him. *A kiss from Cristos was more powerful than any negative ions.*

He smiled. 'Maybe I can tell that to the disgruntled people who are complaining about missing transport connections.'

'You mean suggest they step outside and take a

deep breath? They might not thank you if they're struck by lightning.'

She giggled at the thought of it, and was warmed by Cristos's quiet laughter in return. In another life she might have asked him which of the guests he would like to shove outside on the balcony during a storm. But not here, not now when the room was full of his family and their friends and she was the outsider.

At that moment there was an almighty crack and sheet lightning illuminated the sky and the sea below as if a set of stadium lights had been suddenly switched on. Hayley couldn't help but start in reaction. From behind her came a chorus of squeals from the kids.

Cristos put his hand on her shoulder. She leaned into him without thinking, then pulled away when she realised what she had done. 'Are you frightened?' he asked.

Hayley shook her head. 'When I was tiny I was terrified of storms. It would be a race for who would hide under the bed first—me or my dog. But my father reassured me in much the same way the parents here are doing. "It's just nature's fireworks," he'd say.'

'That's a good way of putting it,' Cristos said. 'I hadn't thought of your banker father as being that lyrical.'

'He has his moments. He was—is—a good father but totally henpecked by my mother. The times when I was out working with him in his shed or building a wall in the garden—things she thought were totally unfeminine—were when we were closest.'

Lightning flashed again. 'Nature's fireworks,' said Cristos. 'I like that description.'

'Magnificent in its own way, isn't it? There are worse things to be frightened of.'

Like loneliness. Despair. Isolation. The feeling of being in an endless dark tunnel with no light ahead to guide her. Feelings she hadn't been able to share with him towards the end of the marriage. Why would she now?

'I guess so,' he said. There was a ragged edge to his voice. Had he suffered when she'd left him? She hadn't thought he would care. Even before her miscarriage she'd begun to believe he wanted out of the marriage. His unexplained long absences, with the nebulous excuse of 'business', on top of the shoots away with the glamorous female models, had had her doubting his commitment. When he hadn't been there for her the day she'd lost the baby, when he had once again said he'd been in a meeting to earn more money for her and the baby without specifying where he had been, her belief in him had been struck a mortal blow.

No. She wouldn't ask how he'd felt when she'd left. She'd always been there to encourage and support him. Until she'd felt so unsupported herself she'd had to go. She'd spent the time since their split building her strength and independence. That independence had been hard won. It had taken her all this time to feel she was ready to face him.

'What was your father like when you were little?' she asked. 'You never talked about him.' She knew he'd been orphaned when he was fourteen but he'd talked more as if Stavros and Penelope had been his parents.

His hand tensed on her shoulder. 'He was away a lot. My mother and I always seemed to be waiting for him to come home.'

His hand slid from her shoulder and for a moment she missed its warmth and strength. 'What about happy father and son memories from when you were little?'

He hesitated. Frowned as if it was a real effort to dredge up the memories. As if he wasn't used to revisiting his childhood. 'I remember him teaching me to fish. When I was about five, I think. Not in the sea. We moved around a lot. In a river with a hand-held line. He was very patient.' He fell silent and Hayley was about to move the conversation on when he spoke. His words were slow and thoughtful as if he was lost in his reminiscence. 'He taught me English. His English was excellent. Heaven knows where he learned it from. I remember him telling me English was the best second language to have. I didn't appreciate it at the time, of course.'

'And you ended up getting a postgraduate degree from one of the top universities in England. Your dad would have been very proud of you.'

He nodded slowly, as if it were a new thought. 'I guess he would.'

Her watch beeped. Silently she cursed it. She wanted to talk more to Cristos about his childhood. But she had made a promise. 'I should go. I volunteered to help Dell in the dining room.'

'Do you need to? You've already done so much work outside,' he said. 'You must be exhausted.'

She remembered how solicitous Cristos had been in the early weeks of her pregnancy. The pregnancy hadn't been planned. But he wouldn't let her refer to it as 'an accident'. Their baby would never feel anything other than wanted and loved, he'd declared. Then he'd used impending father-hood as an excuse to spend more time away from her. He'd said he had to earn as much as possible for his family, that no child of his would ever lack for anything. Looking back, she wondered why she hadn't believed him.

'I like Dell. I feel sorry for her that she's having to run around after everyone when I'm sure she and Alex had more romantic plans for the evening. The catering staff are stuck here like we are and already run off their feet after the celebration lunch. I'm happy to help.'

'Dell will appreciate it. And remember—you're family.'

'Not really,' she said, aghast.

'As far as everyone here is concerned you are my wife. That makes you family,' he said, step-ping closer so no one could overhear, taking up the personal space a husband might expect as his right.

She took a step back, trying not to make it look obvious how shaken she felt by his closeness. 'Family or not, I did promise to help. You know me, I like to keep busy.' She knew she was speaking too fast.

'Yes,' he said. 'I remember.'

Did he still know her? Was she even the same person? She'd never really known him. Not that it had stopped her loving him unconditionally. Looking back, she realised Cristos was very good at being who he thought people wanted him to be. Had seemed to show different facets of himself at different times. What had he kept from her?

By the time Hayley had helped out in the dining room and got back up to the penthouse suite she was exhausted but wide awake. How could she be anything else when she knew Cristos would soon be joining her?

She quickly showered and changed into the new silk pyjamas she'd bought from the resort store. They were tailored man-style, beautifully cut, white and piped around the collar, cuffs and hems in ice blue. She topped them with the plush white velour bath robe she'd found in the closet. There was a matching one in a larger size for Cristos. Couple's robes hanging in a closet for two.

It was very much a couple's room. An enormous king-sized bed dominated, topped with so many pillows it would take her ages just to clear the bed for sleeping. She would never be able to remember how to rearrange them when she made the bed. In the bathroom there were his-and-hers basins, a shower designed for two and a huge free-standing tub.

The spacious suite was all white-veined marble luxury, with pale rugs underfoot and splashes of colour on the walls from the original artworks that seemed to be of the surrounding islands. The balcony doors were closed and shuttered against the storm, but she could imagine it had a spectacular view. The room shrieked 'honeymoon suite', which made it even more of a concern to have to share it with Cristos.

She was so on edge at the thought of him joining her in a honeymoon suite she couldn't settle. In all her plans for the delivery of their divorce documents, she hadn't counted on this.

She paced the marble floor. Fiddled with the television controls with no luck, just a static screen. Examined the contents of the refrigerator—no alcohol, only health drinks. Finally, she lay down on the top of the bed and started to read a novel on her tablet. Useless. She realised she had read the same paragraph three times without absorbing a word. When she heard a bold, loud knock on the door she jumped.

'It's me,' came the deep, masculine voice. *Him.* The door opened. She realised she was clutching the edge of her tablet so tightly she was in danger of cracking it.

The moment he entered the spacious room it seemed smaller. He was so tall and broad-shouldered he seemed to dominate it, to use up more airspace than one man should. Hayley jumped up. She didn't want the fact she was lying on a bed to be misconstrued.

He took a step closer to her, all six feet two of him, in black jeans and a dark charcoal shirt rolled up at the sleeves, his hair a touch dishevelled, the shadow of the day's beard growth darkening his jaw. Without her heeled boots, just the hotel slippers, he towered over her. She felt at a disadvantage in just pyjamas and a robe. She stepped backwards so the edge of the bed pressed against the backs of her legs.

'You're here,' he said. It was the first time they'd been truly alone since she'd arrived on the island.

'Yes.' She looked around her, anywhere but at him. 'I don't know why Alex and Dell gave us such a lovey-dovey room.'

'You know why,' he said shortly. 'They like you and are hoping we'll reconcile.'

'Surely we can ditch the charade now?'

'Absolutely. No need to play games with just the two of us here,' he said. 'In fact, while we're forced into each other's company, it's time for some truths. Starting with why the hell you ran out on me.' His eyes bored into her. At once the practised civility displayed for the wedding renewal guests was dropped. She could sense the anger vibrating from him, extinguishing the traces of their earlier shared intimacy. 'You discharged yourself from hospital without telling me and disappeared. One minute we're married, the next you're gone.'

'You left me alone, terrified, in pain. You switched

off your phone. You weren't working that day. I didn't know where you were.'

'I was in a business meeting. My agent kept calling me and hassling me about some stupid contract detail. I turned the phone off to get him off my back. As soon as I switched it back on I got your messages. I was devastated that I'd missed your calls. You know I got to the hospital as fast as I could. You shouldn't have been on your own and I'll never forgive myself for not being there.'

'All the time I was thinking he'll call me. He'll check in to see how I am. But you never did. I had to go through it all on my own. I felt abandoned.'

'When I got there it was too late.'

'Yes.' She still remembered her agony of despair when the doctor had told her. With no husband by her side.

'If I'd got you to the hospital earlier, could they have saved the baby?'

She couldn't look at him. 'I don't know. Maybe. I don't think so.'

'What caused the miscarriage? You were thirteen weeks—we thought you were safe. I never got to ask you, never found out.'

'They didn't know. The doctors said miscarriage is common in first pregnancies. There was no cause they could identify.' They'd told her to give herself a few months to get over it then try again. But she wasn't going to share that with him.

'I was distraught that we'd lost the baby. Terrified you were so unwell, that I might lose you too. I wanted to comfort you. We should have comforted each other.'

'I wasn't just unwell. I was angry with you. Not just about the phone call. Other things. It all built up.' The days both before and after the miscarriage were a blur; she didn't clearly remember the details. Only her grief and pain.

'What other things? What could have been so bad we couldn't have worked through them? In the beginning we had to fight to be together. We were happy. Then at a time when we should have been there for each other, shared our grief, you ran away. Put yourself right back into the power of your parents, who guarded you from me like rabid watchdogs then spirited you away to Australia. I was your *husband*. Didn't that mean anything? Help me understand why I lost my wife.'

She put up her hand. Had to force her voice to be steady. 'Cristos. Stop right there. I don't want to talk about it. That was the worst time of my life. I took so long to get over it. Reliving it all is too painful.'

He paused. 'I get that. I'm sorry. More sorry than you could know that I wasn't there for you. We won't talk about it if that's what you wish. But can you please fill me in on what you've done in the time we've been apart? You'll be out of here tomorrow. This is our last chance. I know nothing about your life.'

'I guess I owe you that.' She swallowed against a suddenly dry throat. 'I need to get a glass of water first.'

She walked past him, intent on staying a good distance away. So intent she stumbled over the too-big hotel slippers. He caught her arm to steady her.

'No need to be nervous,' he said. 'I'm not going to try to seduce you.' His deep voice, the way his green eyes looked at her as though he could see right through her pyjamas, belied his words. *Why not?* The thought sprung from some wayward corner of her heart.

'I… I didn't think you were going to. That isn't part of the deal,' she said, unable to control the tremor in her voice.

Would it be so bad to have one last fling with him?

It wasn't as if they hadn't made love every night they'd been together of their married life—and often in the day as well. *No!* How did she stop her body from remembering the intense pleasure they had found in each other?

He indicated the white linen sofa that was arranged, with two matching armchairs, around a coffee table carrying an artfully fanned selection of holistic health magazines. 'I told you I'd sleep over there.'

'Thank you,' she said, not sure why she was thanking him. He'd put her in this position. If he hadn't insisted she stay for lunch she would be resting comfortably in her hotel room in Nidri right now, probably checking in online for her flight to Sydney via Dubai.

Or would she?

How well would she have slept just a short boat ride away from Cristos, wondering what he was doing?

'Nice pyjamas,' he said. Was it a subtle re-minder that they had always slept naked entwined in each other's arms? On their wedding night, the night she had lost her virginity, she'd worn a slinky silk nightgown. But he'd peeled it off her and told her there was no need for that—he would keep her warm. And he had. She felt herself flush at the memory of how thrilling it had been and headed to the bar area to get a glass of the filtered water in the fridge. She automatically filled two glasses as she always had during their marriage.

He flung himself down on the sofa that was to be his bed. She placed the glasses on either side of the coffee table, kicked off her slippers and sat down in the chair opposite, drawing her knees up tight. 'What do you want to talk about?' she asked.

'Anything and everything. Finishing your de-gree,' he said. 'How did that happen?'

'As you know, I was close to finishing when I left Durham. But the way we moved around it seemed impossible. Mine weren't the kind of sub-jects you could study in an online podcast from a hotel room in Paris.'

He frowned. 'I didn't mean for it to happen that way. I always felt bad about it.'

'I'm not blaming you. It was a decision we made together.'

For her, there hadn't been a choice between staying behind by herself in Durham while her new husband lived in London or Paris or Milan. Back then, every minute without him had been a minute not lived. He had felt the same. 'We couldn't have done it any other way. But I was never going to be happy without a career of my own.'

'Granted,' he said.

'I got credit for my studies at Durham and was admitted to the degree at the University of New South Wales. I fell on my feet.'

'And found a job.'

'While I was at uni I did an internship with a solar energy company. They asked me to get in touch when I graduated. So I did.'

Cristos picked up his glass of water and put it down again without drinking any. 'All this time you were living a completely different life, one I can't even imagine,' he said slowly. 'What about the guy back there?'

'He's a friend,' she said.

'A friend with benefits?' he said tersely.

'No! We haven't even dated.' Now it was her turn to pick up her glass, take a sip of water to moisten a suddenly dry mouth. 'But he's nice. And who knows what might happen after I'm divorced?' She looked down at the glass.

'There must have been other men.'

'No,' she said. 'I wasn't interested.'

'I find that difficult to believe,' he said.

Now she looked up to meet his gaze full on. There was no point in talking in circles. 'I was in a very bad way after losing the baby. Dating was the last thing on my mind.'

His eyes narrowed. 'Are you telling me...?'

'There hasn't been anyone since you. There wasn't anyone before you. There's only been you, Cristos. Legally I'm still married to you. I couldn't sleep with another man while I was still your wife. It wouldn't have been right.' And she hadn't wanted it—hadn't wanted another man touching her. It had been too soon, she had rationalised.

Cristos made an inarticulate sound deep in his throat. 'I thought... I imagined...' He choked out the words.

She realised she hadn't actually given a thought to Tim since she'd set eyes on Cristos again. Tim, who would be waiting at the airport in Sydney to meet her like the good friend that he was. The kind man who had tried to kiss her and she had pushed him away.

Because he wasn't Cristos.

'What about you?' she said. 'Freed from that inconvenient wife. What about that gorgeous American model who was always hanging about? Ginny. I felt sure you and her—' She put up her hand. 'Don't answer that. I don't want to know. I really couldn't bear to hear about you with someone else. Even…even when I don't want you for myself.'

In turn he held up his right hand, his fingers splayed to display his wide gold wedding band. 'I didn't take this off. I still considered myself married to you. That meant being faithful to my wife. Like I always was when we were together. There haven't been other women for me. From the moment I met you in the pub in Durham, there was only ever you.'

Hayley wasn't often lost for words but she struggled to breathe, let alone speak. Silence hung between them for a long moment. 'That can't be true,' she managed to choke out.

'Believe it,' he said.

'Not Ginny? I felt sure—' Never had she felt shorter or more wide-hipped than in the presence of tall, rangy Ginny.

'I talked business with Ginny. Nothing else.'

'That last morning, she called the apartment wanting to speak to you.'

'About nothing but a deal I was discussing with her,' he said dismissively. It had sounded more than that to Hayley but she hadn't exactly been in a good frame of mind. Besides, this was hardly the time to argue it.

'No Ginny, no one else? But you're such a sexy man. And all those women wanting you. Even here today.'

'I'm certainly not celibate for lack of offers. Perhaps I've been a fool. Staying faithful to a wife who didn't want me. *Who ran away.*' He turned his wedding band around and around his finger.

She hadn't expected this. Not in a million years had she expected this. Believing he had been unfaithful was one of the reasons she had hardened her heart towards him. Feeling ill, cramping, in pain, unable to reach her husband to help her, she had imagined him with another woman, with Ginny's lithe limbs wrapped around him.

His green eyes infinitely sad, Cristos started to slide off his wedding ring.

Hayley's mind was reeling. Her intake of breath was so swift it came out as a gasp. 'No!' she said. 'Not now.' She reached over to stay his hand. 'Time enough for that tomorrow. You take off your ring. I take off mine. Then we say goodbye.'

CHAPTER SEVEN

FOR MORE THAN two years Cristos had been torturing himself with thoughts of Hayley with another man.

But she had stayed true to him.

He could scarcely believe it. He wondered at her reasons. But he didn't doubt her. To his knowledge, Hayley had never lied to him. He rode a great surge of exultation that rushed through his heart.

He was still her only lover.

Surely that meant something. He pushed his wedding ring firmly back into place. Perhaps, if he played his cards right, there could be a chance it would stay there. Because he still wanted her.

It took all the self-control he could muster not to sweep her into his arms and kiss her—properly this time. Not some polite charade of a kiss for the benefit of observers. A hungry, passionate kiss that was a prelude to possessing her, to reminding her why no other man would ever make her body sing the way he could.

Instead he relied on his gambler's instincts and waited to see what she might say next.

Being in a hotel room alone together gave a false sense of intimacy. But the coffee table was a barrier between them. Hayley leaned against the back of her chair, as if to emphasise the distance, perhaps to give him the impression she was relaxed. But her shoulders hunched defensively and she nervously twisted the ends of the hotel robe's tie without seeming to realise she was doing so.

She seemed swamped by the robe—a generic size designed for a woman less petite. It gave little hint of her slim, shapely body. The thick fabric wrapped over her breasts up to her neck, fell down past her knees. Her hair framed her face in tiny, damp tendrils—that short, short hair he was still getting used to. With her face free of make-up she looked very young. He had only two years on her but he felt infinitely older.

Finally, she stopped fiddling with the tie of her robe. She looked up at him, her blue eyes clouded. 'How did we get here, Cristos?' She had always called him by his Greek name, had never shortened and anglicised it to Chris or lengthened it to Christopher as some of his English friends had done.

He knew she didn't mean here in Greece, here on this island. 'I don't have an answer for you. But here we are. In the same room. Speaking to each other. Trying to make sense of our past.'

She jumped up from her chair, paced its length and back again. She rested her forehead in the heels of her hands, her fingers clutching her hair, then dropped them to look up at him. Her hair was tousled, her eyes red rimmed. 'I'm confused.'

Cristos kept a poker face as he got up to stand near her. 'Confused in what way?' He had to tread cautiously, as if through a field of landmines.

She flung out her hands. 'This isn't how it was meant to be. You. Me. Getting trapped here with you. Pretending we're still together. I intended to give you the divorce documents and then be gone. To put our marriage behind us. But then you threw a curve ball—that you haven't been with another woman. I'm reeling from your revelation. You see, I thought there must have been another woman in Milan, if not Ginny someone else. Maybe more than one.'

He frowned. 'Because I'm a man? That my gender makes me predisposed to cheat? Despite our marriage vows? You insult me. I loved you, Hayley. There was no other woman. I didn't want anyone else.'

'I so want to believe you. But it's difficult for me to believe there weren't women flinging themselves at you, Mr Sexiest Man in Europe.' He had hated that name—bestowed on him by one of the international gossip magazines.

'Of course there were,' he said. 'Thousands of them. More than one man could possibly handle.'

That forced a reluctant hint of a smile. 'Really.'

'What did you call yourself earlier? An "inconvenient wife"? I never saw you as that. I didn't want anyone but you. Even after you ran away. But you didn't want to be found.' He hadn't thought of searching for her somewhere as far-flung as Australia.

'No, I didn't.' Her face drooped; lines of weariness bracketed her mouth.

He chose his next words carefully. 'So, I didn't date.'

'But you're such a sexy man.'

'I'm also a man of self-control. Once we are

divorced it will, of course, be different. I won't want to stay alone.'

Her mouth thinned. 'Of course.'

'Though how I'll choose from among those thousands of women, I'm not sure. I might have to run auditions.'

Hayley stifled a little whimper that tore at his heart. 'That isn't funny,' she said.

He took a step closer, so close he could breathe in her warm, freshly showered scent—lemon and thyme from the hotel's artisan soap and shampoo overlaid the essential sweet scent of his wife. 'I'm sorry. That was a joke in bad taste. The truth is once we split for good, I will find someone else.'

He wanted her to deny the divorce. To say that after seeing him again she didn't want to go through with it after all. But she didn't. And the flame of his optimism flickered and dimmed.

'I… I suppose so.' But her uncertainty made him wonder about the guy in Sydney. How serious she was about him. Was there really another player in the game?

'That is, if you are still determined to go ahead with the divorce.'

She tilted her chin upward and met his eyes

defiantly, but then betrayed herself by biting down on her lower lip. 'Yes. I am. That's why I came here. You want it too.'

'We could always change our minds,' he said. He gripped the tops of her arms and looked down into her face, urging her to give him the answer he wanted. She stilled under his touch; if she'd attempted to move away he would have let her go. But she didn't.

For a long moment she looked back up at him, her blue eyes clouded with uncertainty. *He had to kiss her.* To taste her sweet mouth, to try to communicate with touch what words could not. He drew her close, felt the warmth of her body through the cool silk of her pyjamas, her slender curves. He smoothed a thumb along her jaw, learning the feel of her soft skin again, traced the outline of her lips. She shuddered a little and he stopped. Then he dipped his head, brushed his lips gently against hers. Nothing too demanding. Nothing too passionate. He wanted her so desperately with the pent-up longing of years but he didn't want to scare her off.

She stayed rigid, as if bracing herself against her own response. Her breathing quickened but still she stayed still. *She wasn't ready.* Reluctantly he drew away. He wouldn't let her sense his disappointment.

Then suddenly *she* was kissing *him*. She pulled his head down to hers, pressed her mouth urgently against his, whimpered her need. He drew her to him again and kissed her back. Her tongue slipped into his mouth, he met it with his and they danced the familiar dance as if there hadn't been years since their last real kiss. He slid his hands down her back, pulled her closer. His optimism flamed back into life as if she had thrown accelerant on his hopes.

Then Hayley abruptly pulled away. Her face flushed, eyes dilated, her mouth swollen. She looked down to the floor. 'No. We can't do this.' She drew in her breath in a sob. Finally, after what seemed an age but was probably only seconds, she looked up, her expression determined. 'I'm sorry, Cristos. That wasn't fair of me.'

'Not fair? In what way?' he choked out. *Fair* wasn't the way to describe the dynamics of that kiss. He struggled to get his breath back on an even keel.

'I thought I'd talked myself out of my attraction to you,' she said. 'But it's still there. I still want you.'

And that was something to worry about?

'I've never stopped wanting you.' He felt fired by an urgency to reassure her. But she put up one small, pale hand to stop him. He knew that look of old—a 'but' was certain to follow.

'But that isn't enough. There has to be more than great sex to make a marriage, to make a family.'

He had to stamp on a cynical laugh. Hayley spoke as if 'great sex' were something casually acquired—almost to be disparaged. She'd been untouched when she'd come to him. Did she really have no idea of how rare that perfect sexual connection they'd shared from the start was between a man and a woman? She'd had no other man to compare—but surely she'd be aware of how special it was?

He frowned. 'I don't know where you're coming from. Yes, we had great sex. But we had so much more than that. We had each other's backs. We were life partners.' His marriage to Hayley had given him everything that had been missing from his life—love, security, his own place in the world as her husband and, he'd hoped, the father of their child.

She drew her mouth in a tight line. '*Had* being the operative word. Past tense. We started off brilliantly. But then things changed.'

'Of course they did. We moved to different countries. I switched career. We grew up.'

She made an impatient gesture as if waving away his words. 'I didn't mean that. I meant we started off equals. Both sitting on the same perch making the decisions that affected us both. Talking things over if we disagreed. Making compromises.'

'That's right, we did,' he said, puzzled as to why she would bring that up.

'Then it seemed all the compromises were one way. Made by me.'

Behind the sweetness was a toughness in her stance, the way she stood with legs braced, a simmering aggression—as if a fluffy kitten had grown spikes like a porcupine. He frowned. 'The way I remember it, we both made compromises.'

She shook her head. 'I remember it differently. The first thing to go was my career. Big compromise. There wasn't much I could do without completing my degree. Maybe in London I could have got a halfway decent job. Even in Paris I spoke enough French to get work waitressing. Thank heaven for that gap year I spent working as an *au pair* in the south of France. But I didn't speak a word of Italian. By the time we got to Milan I was pretty much a housewife. Just Mrs Theofanis. Housewife to a husband who was never there. Who kept me in ignorance about where he was, what he was doing. Not to mention the fact that you actually had a wife was a deep, dark secret.'

He spread out his hands like an open book. 'You knew where I was when I was on assignments.'

'What about when you were "doing business"? I didn't know where you were or who you were with. I felt I was pushed down rung by rung off that perch beside you until I found myself scrabbling on the ground below.' There was a note of anger, of bitterness he had never heard before. Or perhaps he had never listened.

Cristos closed his eyes. 'I had no idea you felt that way.'

That was when he realised the first mistake he'd made. Choosing not to tell her the risks he was taking. Hiding from her the fact he'd knocked back lucrative modelling jobs so he could work on his own investments. Not when security had seemed so very important to her. 'Everything I did was for you, for us.'

Hayley played again with the tie on her dressing gown, twisting it tightly around her fingers like a tourniquet. 'I wish I could believe that. Seemed to me the marriage became all about you.'

He cursed under his breath. Not at her. At himself. 'You know I never wanted you to be a "secret wife".'

Her voice softened. 'I know. But it went on for too long. I began to feel invisible to you as well as to your fans.' She dropped her eyes down to where her bare toes were making a small circle in the rug. 'From invisible I began to feel inadequate.'

'Koukla.' He went to reach for her but she twisted away to evade his touch.

'If you think you can kiss me into submission, forget it,' she said. 'That won't work any more.'

'I didn't want to kiss you. No. I've always wanted to kiss you. I wanted to apologise. To say how sorry I am that you felt that way and that I didn't know.'

The modelling. That disruptive lifestyle. The pressures on him—and on her. It all came down to that. Again he cursed. How many times had he wished he had never showed Hayley the model scout's business card? Yet he'd been able to piggyback on the good money he'd earned to make a fortune.

'I understood that,' she said. 'You blame the modelling career for what went wrong between us. In some part, I agree.'

'That's when things changed between us.' He spoke the words leadenly.

'Not in the beginning. It was amusing then, a novelty. The parties were fun too, places we'd never been, people we would never have met. A lifestyle neither of us could ever have imagined. But the more popular you got, the more I got left behind.' She turned so he could only see her in profile. 'I got to hate your job. But I never wanted to tell you that. You loved it and it was so very well paid.'

Cristos abruptly turned from her, then swung back. '*You* got to hate it? Not half as much as I hated it.'

Her eyes widened in disbelief. 'What do you

mean? I thought you loved being the man of the moment? A star.'

'I loved the money being a model brought us. The opportunities it gave us. In the beginning, some of the jobs were a buzz. But much of it I found demeaning. Not to mention just plain boring. I was a commodity. The director and photographer discuss you as if you're not present. On a shoot they push and pull you into place as if you're some kind of store mannequin, not a person. If I didn't know my nose cast the wrong kind of shadow before, I sure knew it after. And to my traditional family to be a model means a man must be gay—'

'Do you remember my parents asked me if you were gay when I told them what you were doing?' she asked. 'And how I laughed at the idea of it.'

'Constant slurs on my masculinity got more difficult to laugh off.'

'I didn't realise,' she said.

'You can imagine what my grandparents thought. Having their grandson splashed over billboards in his underpants was not, in their opinion, a worthy job for a Greek man with my education. If my *yia-yia* could have got a can of black paint and got up on a ladder to mask me out of those adverts she would have. Of course I heard all this after I came home—their disappointment in me spelled out in excruciating detail.'

'I'm so sorry to hear that. But forgive me for smiling at the thought of your grandmother with her bucket of paint, scrambling up the buildings in Times Square in New York with her paint-brush.'

'She would have been very busy. The posters were everywhere.'

'You looked darn good on those billboards,' she said. 'Mr Sexiest Man in Europe all right. At the time, your agent told me sales of those underpants rocketed all around the world.'

'The underwear people weren't happy when I refused an encore performance. They couldn't believe I would walk away from such a lucrative contract.'

'So why did you walk away?'

'Without you there, what was the point? I was fed up with some of the temperamental people I was forced to work with. The pressure to stay in peak form. Living in Italy and not able to eat what I wanted. All those hours at the gym keeping in shape. No wonder so many of the models—male and female—had eating disorders.'

'Those hours at the gym weren't a bad thing.'

He was aware of her not so covert inspection of his body, fitter and stronger even than when she'd last seen him. He liked to keep active. At first he'd pounded through the gym out of anger and despair and frustration. Forcing his body into submission to banish thoughts of Hayley. Back here on the islands, he'd found again the things he'd loved like swimming and running, hitting the gym for enjoyment rather than punishment. He had to counteract with physical activity the long hours he spent at a desk managing his wide-ranging investments.

'Modelling was a means to an end,' he said. 'I never saw it as a career. Rather a way to get some money together before we started our real lives.'

'I thought that was your real life. And that there was no place in that life for me.'

How could he have allowed her to think that? So maybe he had been dazzled by the so-called glamour of it all to start. He'd been so young, fresh out of uni. And there had been good times. But nothing could have made up for going home to the empty apartment. When he'd cleared it, he'd found tucked away in the back of a drawer a little knitted yellow hat Hayley must have bought in anticipation of the baby. For a long time he had stood with it held to his face. Only when he'd gone to put it away had he found he had wet it with tears he hadn't known he had shed.

He cleared his throat. 'You couldn't have been more wrong. I did it for you. For our future. Once you were out of the picture there was no incentive to keep on pushing myself in a role I'd grown to loathe.'

And by then he'd found a more lucrative way to make money, one that satisfied him intellectually and fed his gambler's soul. He couldn't deny the rush when a gamble paid off—but unlike his father he had weighed up risks with an acute business brain. The apps had kicked it off. Then he'd gone on to invest in property, industry, even a successful West End musical.

'I was surprised when I heard that you came back to your childhood home. I thought you might have gone to Athens. Got a job there.'

'I was in no frame of mind to do that. Not when all my efforts were directed into finding my wife.

I hunted for you, Hayley. But met a dead end everywhere I looked.'

'When did you give up?' she asked in a very small voice.

'When your mother decided to take one of my regular but usually unanswered calls and informed me that you were perfectly healthy, perfectly happy and did not want to see me ever again. After two years I talked to my lawyer about divorce.'

'I'm sorry. About my mother, I mean. She was overly protective. I'm also sorry you didn't get to use your business degree.'

He gave a short bark of laughter. 'Don't be sorry about that. I'm my own boss. I like it that way.'

Her forehead pleated into a frown. 'Is ferrying people on your boat enough? You're a very smart man, Cristos.'

He should tell her now how wealthy he was. But then he would have to tell her about the secrets buried in his past, the risks he had taken, his fears, the insecurities he had never wanted to admit to her. 'The boat is a hobby. Relaxation. If I can help people out with a ride between islands that's good too. But I don't earn my living as a boatman.'

'How you earn your living isn't actually any of my business now. But you got used to a certain standard of living with what you earned. I'd hate to see you go backwards.'

'My investments make me a more than good enough living. That's what the business meetings in Milan were about. I'd made some good contacts. I was looking to the future.'

Their future.

Hayley was more relieved than she could have imagined to hear that Cristos was doing okay. They'd had such a struggle at the start. The modelling career had seemed like a godsend.

But she was astounded to discover how much he'd hated it. Why hadn't she known that? Had she really listened when he'd come home exhausted and complaining about some tyrannical fashion director? She'd wanted so much to be a support to him, as her mother had never been to her father, yet it seemed she had failed. Even before her pregnancy had brought on its problems and changed everything.

'What about you?' he said.

'Sydney is an expensive city to live in. But I'm sharing an apartment with a very nice girl and doing okay. I really like my job. People only know me there as Hayley Clements. Not as the appendage of a dominant male.'

His face contorted with what looked like real concern, pain and a good dose of anguish. But, Cristos being Cristos, he only looked more handsome. Dark and brooding suited him. Dark and brooding had brought him a lot of work. Although she'd loved him most when he was laughing, those fabulous white teeth against his warm olive skin, his green eyes sparkling with good humour.

'I'm gutted you thought you were in any way lesser,' he said now. 'I blame myself entirely.' A bleak shadow darkened his eyes. 'If I could turn back the clock I would. Especially to the night we lost our baby.'

Hayley tensed. 'I told you I didn't want to talk any more about that.'

To talk further about her miscarriage meant having to reveal more of her life afterwards. The deep, dark depression that had overwhelmed her. That had worried her parents so much they had admitted her to a clinic. The long struggle back from those black depths.

'I'm sorry,' he said.

'I'm sorry too,' she said. 'Looking back, I didn't realise the pressures on you. My only excuse is that I was young, inexperienced and maybe not ready to be a wife.'

'I wasn't much older. Maybe neither of us was ready. Maybe we—'

'Should have got to know each other better before we—'

'Dived into that shark pool of the modelling world.'

'It was a shark pool, wasn't it? Seething with vicious creatures, jaws open and snapping with razor-sharp teeth. Your agent, some of those bookers, even the clients. They were predators.'

'And we were naïve, fresh prey,' he said.

'Now, a few years on, I wouldn't put up with being made a secret wife hiding in your shadow. Not for a moment.'

'I wouldn't have allowed it. I didn't want to allow it then. I should have trusted my instincts.'

Hayley's instincts were begging to be heard

right now. Go to him. Put your arms around him. Hold him close.

Don't let him go again.

But her instincts had seen her give up her life for him. Her intellect told her to hang on to her independence.

She yawned. A genuine yawn. But she exaggerated it. 'Bed time,' she said, then immediately regretted her choice of words. 'I mean…well, I don't mean—'

'Bed time for you. Sofa time for me. I get it.'

She clutched her robe closer to her. 'Uh. Okay. Do you need to use the bathroom?'

'No. You go,' he said.

When she came back into the room, he had changed out of his jeans and shirt, and was wearing his boxers and a white T-shirt. He'd pulled a sheet, blanket and a pillow from the closet and was throwing them across the sofa.

Her mouth went dry at the sight of him in so little clothing. He was cut, every muscle honed. In even better shape than when she'd last seen him like this. For some of his jobs he'd had to wax away all his body hair. She'd never liked it.

Now he had just the right amount of dark hair on his chest, his legs, that she had found so exciting.

How could one man be so perfect?

'I…well, I'll say goodnight.'

He looked up. 'Goodnight, Hayley.'

For a long moment their gazes met. 'Does this seem seriously weird to you?' she said.

'Yeah. It does. This morning I had no idea I'd ever see you again. Now we're sharing a room. But I'm glad you're here. Happy we could talk.'

'Me too.' *He had not been with another woman.*

He lay down on the sofa, pulled the blanket over him and rolled away from her. He pummelled his pillow into place—as he had always done. Only that had been after they'd made love and she'd snuggled beside him and used his chest as her pillow. Now all she could see was his broad shoulders and the back of his dark head. 'You can turn the lights off from the switches by the bed,' he said.

She made her way over to the big, empty bed. Slid into the cool sheets. Resisted the urge to pummel her pillow because that was what he'd done. Reached over to fumble for the light switch.

Then lay on her back and stared at the ceiling. Sleep would never come.

But it must have.

She awoke with a start. Didn't know where she was for a moment. Saw by the light from the bedside clock it was past midnight.

The bed seemed very big and empty. She'd barely made a bump in the bed linen. Outside the wind had dropped completely and it seemed utterly quiet and perfectly still. So still, it felt scary. As her eyes adjusted to the gloom she could see Cristos, illuminated by the faint light from the clock and the glow from the standby light on the television, as he lay on the sofa just steps away from her bed.

She could hear the rustling of the sheet as he turned. Then turned again. His breathing was too loud for him to be asleep. He bashed the pillow with his fist and crashed back onto the sofa as if he were diving into a belly flop. Definitely awake.

Hayley sat up, resting on her elbows so she could better see him. One long, muscular leg was hanging off the sofa from under the covers. His arm trailed the floor. He turned again but it was obvious the sofa was much too small for him to be comfortable. Or rather he was too big. She was so much smaller than him. She would fit better. The sofa should be hers.

She swung her legs to the floor. Made her way over to him. 'Cristos,' she whispered. He pretended to be asleep and didn't reply. 'I know you're awake,' she said in her normal voice.

'I'm trying to sleep,' he mumbled.

'You're never going to get to sleep on that sofa,' she said. 'It's too small. You take the bed. Let me take the sofa.'

'I'm fine,' he protested.

'You're not.' She pulled the sheet off him. Gasped. His T-shirt had ridden up to show his hard chest, his perfect six-pack. 'Give me the sofa.'

He snatched back the sheet. 'No.'

She sighed. 'This is ridiculous. Neither of us is going to get any sleep.'

He dropped his guard momentarily as he lifted his head to face her. She took her chance and grabbed both sheet and blanket from him. 'You'll freeze without them.'

'A gentleman takes the sofa,' he said.

'I don't know in what guidebook to chivalry that's written,' she said.

'You wouldn't know—girls don't read them,' he said. 'Besides, my copy is written in Greek. Ancient Greek. In Cyrillic script.'

She smiled and rolled her eyes, even though he couldn't see her. 'So we'll share the bed.'

'Not a good idea,' he said.

'It's the size of a tennis court,' she said. 'You stay your side and I'll stay mine. We could put a barricade of pillows down the middle if you'd like. Now get up, please. I can't sleep knowing how uncomfortable you must be on that sofa. You've got a big day ahead of you tomorrow ferrying people over to Nidri.'

'You always were a bossy little thing,' he said with a mock groan.

Not bossy enough, she thought. Knowing what she now knew about their time in Milan she might have done things differently. If she'd asserted herself more she might not have grown so insecure about her husband. Might not have constantly compared herself to the beautiful women he worked with and found herself lacking.

'Come on,' she said. 'I need my sleep too.'

He rolled off the sofa. Stretched. Her heart stopped at the splendour of him. Could she really sleep in the same bed as him and not want to jump his bones? Ill-advised as that might be? He staggered towards the bed, pretending, she thought, to be drowsier than he was.

She'd always slept on his left. Nearer to his heart, he'd said as he'd pulled her close. Now they fell into the marriage-allotted sides of the bed without question. Only he was as far to the edge as possible on his side and she the same on hers. He turned his back to her. She did the same. Was he thinking the same jumping-the-bones thing she was?

'That's much more comfortable for you,' she said. 'Goodnight.'

'G'night,' he said, in a voice that already sounded half asleep. But she knew he was feigning sleep and she was glad. It made the awkward situation so much easier. Maybe she should wait until he fell asleep and then creep over to the sofa.

Stay where she was and she would probably lie there rigidly unable to sleep, conscious of his presence in her bed for the first time in two and a half years. But it happened the opposite way. Just knowing she wasn't alone in the bed, that Cristos was there, made her relax and she was asleep before she'd even had a chance to worry about not being able to fall asleep.

The next time she woke, it was very early morning, a hint of grey pre-dawn light creeping through the shutters. For a moment she didn't know where she was. A warm, male *familiar* body was spooned against her back, his arm flung around her waist, his hand resting on her hip. *Cristos.*

She stilled. Breathed in his scent, felt the warm whisper of his breath on her skin, the subtle scratch of his beard. Cristos was right. It hadn't just been about sex with them. After they'd had sex they would lie like this to go to sleep. It had also been about comfort, reassurance, *love*.

Why had they let it go?

It was dangerous to stay here like this. It would be too easy to turn in his arms, to wake him with kisses, to slide off his clothes—and hers. To open her body to him—and risk opening her heart. What if he were to plant tiny kisses on the sensitive nape of her neck? What if his hand slipped upwards to cup her breast? In the past they had indulged in a morning delight whenever they'd had a chance. But it couldn't happen. She should edge away from him and hit that sofa. But she would allow herself just one more minute with him. And another. Until she couldn't bear to leave his embrace and drowsiness overwhelmed her.

CHAPTER EIGHT

HAYLEY WOKE TO a cold morning light flooding through the open doors of the balcony. And a cold morning breeze wafting towards the bed that made her shiver and tug the duvet over her shoulders.

The glass doors to the balcony had been flung open. Cristos stood framed by the doorway, looking out to sea with his back to her and his arms outstretched, as if making a homage to the morning. He wore just his T-shirt and boxers. Broad shoulders tapered to a narrow waist and the best butt she had ever seen on a man. Not that she had ever actually seen another man's butt clad in just underwear—knit cotton boxers that emphasised hard male buttocks and muscular thighs—to compare but she could not believe any other man could compete. It was a fine view to wake up to.

She reached out a hand to the rumpled sheets beside her. The high-thread-count linen was still warm. He must not be long out of bed—her side of the bed.

She had slept the night with her soon-to-be-ex-husband.

How warm and comforting it had been with him spooned against her. Yet she was glad it had not led to more. Today she would be flying more than fifteen thousand kilometres back to her life in Sydney.

Cristos would like Sydney.

Perhaps he could come visit. Perhaps—

'You're awake.' Cristos turned to face her. 'Come see.'

The doors to the balcony had been shuttered the night before. Yes, she would like to see the view. She checked to see if her pyjama top had slid open in the night then slipped into her robe and the too-big slippers before heading to join him.

It was the first time she had seen Cristos in the morning for a long, long time. Her heart flipped over inside her at the sight of his handsome, once so beloved face.

His black hair was all ruffled and standing up in peaks. She had to shove her hands in her dressing-gown pockets to stop herself from reaching up to smooth it into place. His beard had grown overnight to shadow his jaw, a look she had always found incredibly sexy. She ached to stroke the roughness that contrasted with his smooth olive skin elsewhere, but kept her hands fisted firmly in her pockets. His extraordinary green eyes, framed with thick black lashes, still looked sleepy, half lidded and sensual.

This was *her* Cristos. Not the Cristos she'd had to share with his fans. The man no one else saw, though they'd strived to give a taste of intimate, early-morning bedroom Cristos in countless photographic shoots and commercials. The captured images had come nowhere near the heart-rendingly beautiful reality of the man.

For a moment, she thought he was going to lean down and kiss her and she was unsure how she would react.

Kiss him back and drag him over to the bed?

But the moment passed. Cristos stood aside to give her access to the balcony. Icy air needled her face. She soon saw the reason why. 'Snow,' she breathed. 'It's beautiful. Not what I ever expected to see on a Greek island.'

'It's not usual here,' he said. 'I told you, this is the coldest winter I can remember.'

Heavy snow had fallen overnight and flakes still drifted slowly down. The balcony and its railings were frosted with it. She leaned forward to see as much as she could without venturing out onto the balcony in flimsy slippers and risking frostbite.

Ahead of her was the sea, below the curve of the beach, and to each side forested hillsides that sloped down to the water. Everywhere but the water itself was covered in white. The trees. The beach. The boats moored at the resort dock. It was magical. A fairy-tale landscape. 'You could make snowmen on the beach,' she said, reaching up to catch snowflakes in her hands.

'No doubt the kids will be doing just that very soon,' he said.

She pivoted to face him. 'But we'll all be leaving this morning.'

'I doubt that,' he said, leaning back against the doorframe.

'What do you mean?'

'Look at the sea,' he said, indicating the white-foamed, choppy waters. Blue sky was struggling through gaps in the clouds but the sea still looked wild and forbidding.

She shivered. 'But you said we could leave today.'

'Weather permitting was always the proviso.'

'And you're telling me the weather is saying "no way".'

'I'm afraid so. Even if we could get off the island, the roads will be closed, as will the causeway that links Lefkada to the mainland. They might have lost power in Nidri.'

'You mean I'm still stuck here? For how long?'

'Indefinitely, I suggest,' he said. Was that a grin hovering around his mouth?

'How will I get to the airport?' she said, knowing how ridiculous the question sounded as soon as it left her mouth. 'The airport will most likely be closed too, won't it?'

'Most likely,' he said.

Her voice rose with the panic that gripped her. 'I'm meant to fly to Dubai this afternoon.'

'I wouldn't count on that,' he said.

'Damn! One night I could manage but this. Trapped here indefinitely. It's unbearable.'

'You're welcome to stay here as long as you

want.' The grin burst into full, disarming life. 'Not that you have any choice.'

She stared at him. 'You're glad about this.'

'Guilty as charged. Fate has dealt me an unexpected good hand. More time together.' His eyes narrowed. 'Maybe a second chance with you.'

A second chance.

Her heart gave a betraying little leap at his words. But she shook her head. 'It's way too late to consider that.'

He pounced. 'So you have considered it?'

Kissing him. Lying in that honeymoon bed with him so close. The thought had crossed her mind, in a 'what if?' kind of way. 'No. That's crazy talk,' she said. 'We're strangers to each other now.'

He frowned. 'Do you really think so? That there's nothing left of the people we used to be?'

'I've changed since we were together. I'm sure you have too. We hurt each other in the past. One conversation isn't enough to heal those old hurts.'

'We can have more conversations.' His gaze was intent.

Her heart skipped a beat with panic. 'Please don't put pressure on me.'

For a long moment he looked down at her. She

felt her body stirring at his closeness. The only man who had ever made her feel like this. But she had to protect herself. Her life now was ordered and stable, not the wild swings life had been with Cristos. And that stability had been hard won.

'No pressure,' he said finally. 'I'm just asking you to give our marriage a second chance.'

'And I'm telling you I can't do that. It's been less than twenty-four hours.'

'I still want you. You can't blame me for trying.' Maybe she would have been insulted if he hadn't. As she'd told him before, she was confused about her reactions to him.

'We could try to get to know each other again while I'm trapped here on the island,' she said.

'Why do I feel I've been handed the booby prize?' he said. 'But I'll play it your way.'

'Thank you,' she said with relief and a curious sense of anticipation. 'So, what will happen at the resort now? This room. Will we stay in here?'

'I'm sure Dell and Alex will expect people to remain in their allocated rooms. You stay here.

But I'm going to bunk down with my grandparents in their room.'

She stared at him. 'Why? There's plenty of room here. I'll take the sofa tonight.'

His face tensed. 'I cannot sleep another night in the same room as you, and certainly not in the same bed, without making love to you. It's too much to ask of a man. Self-control can only go so far.'

'It was difficult for me too,' she said.

'Don't tell me that,' he groaned. 'It makes it worse.'

She couldn't look at him, scared of what she might see, how she might react. 'What will people think about us in separate rooms?'

'Who will know?'

'Your grandparents might have an idea if you're planning to be in their room. What will you tell them?'

'That you couldn't put up with my snoring and kicked me out.'

'But you don't snore.'

'I hope not. But that's beside the point. If you can think of a better excuse, tell me. I don't want to tell them the truth.'

She smiled. 'I doubt Penelope would want the X-rated reason.' He rolled his eyes in the way she had always found endearing. 'What about the others?' she said. 'Do we keep up the pretence?'

'It would be easier than making awkward explanations at this stage.'

'I think so too,' she said. They were on such friendlier terms it didn't seem such a sham.

He glanced at his watch. 'The place is probably in an uproar with interrupted travel plans. I'll get dressed, head down to the office and look at the weather reports on the internet. There's WiFi in this room. Better check your phone for airline information on your flights.'

'I'll do that,' she said, turning to head back into the room.

He caught her by the arm to stop her. Turned her to face him. She looked up into that handsome face she had once loved so much. His eyes seemed to do an inventory of her features, as if memorising them. 'I want to know you better, Hayley,' he said in that deep voice. His slight accent became more pronounced, as it had used to in times of deep emotion.

She caught her breath. 'Me too. I mean, know you better.'

Within minutes he had gone, leaving Hayley alone and realising the room felt very empty indeed without him.

For nearly two and a half years Cristos had been haunted by his last sight of Hayley, pale and drawn in that hospital bed. He'd let her down and he'd paid the price.

She had changed. It wasn't just the hair. It was the demeanour too. He liked that she was tougher, stronger, particularly as he wasn't around to look after her any more.

He'd always wanted to look after her and protect her. On their wedding day he'd made an extra, private vow. He would never treat his wife the way his father had treated his mother.

His father hadn't looked after his mother the way she'd deserved. He'd left her and himself as a child to fend for themselves while he was incarcerated. Then done nothing to mend his ways to avoid another prison sentence. Thankfully his grandparents had always welcomed his mother back to Nidri. But the welcome had not been without conditions—his mother had to be always grateful, never rock the boat and have a feasible story to explain why her husband was away on business for so long. Then, acting against all the family's advice, she had always gone back to him, taking Cristos with her, until the time had come that he'd had to stay with his grandparents in term time to ensure some continuity of his education.

He saw, now, that he took after his mother as much as his father. She had been a one-man woman, never giving up on the husband she'd loved and married against all advice. He was the same with Hayley. He'd wanted only her from the time he'd met her. No other woman had interested him. He'd persisted in his search for her long after he should have given up on her. He didn't intend to give up now.

CHAPTER NINE

IT WOULD BE so easy to fall in love with Cristos again, Hayley thought. *Too easy.* Memories of how caring he could be wrapped around her with the same enveloping warmth as his body had provided, spooning hers last night. He had been everything she'd wanted before things between them had gone so wrong.

After the miscarriage and her spiral into depression, she'd been forced to protect herself by putting a lid on her good memories of her husband. But the seal was beginning to loosen.

Here on Kosmimo, she'd begun to recognise glimpses of the old Cristos—the man she'd vowed to love 'until death do us part'.

Not that those words had been spoken in the ceremony that had united them in law as man and wife. They'd murmured them to each other later, in the privacy of the big four-poster bed in a bed and breakfast near Durham where they'd spent their wedding night. Her new husband had wanted to make her first time special. He hadn't thought that likely in her cramped room in the student house in the Viaduct.

Cristos had been tender, patient and passionate. The pleasure he had brought her to had been so intense she had fallen apart in tears afterwards. She had sobbed, not because it had hurt—though it had a little—but in wonder and appreciation of the perfectly splendid man she had married. After that, each time they'd made love had been more memorable than the last as they'd grown to know each other's wants and needs.

He'd been surprised when she'd first told him she was a virgin and wanted to stay so until she got married. At twenty-two, she'd been a rarity. Gradually he'd got the story of why she'd taken such a stance. Her mother had fallen pregnant to her father at age nineteen. She'd 'had' to get married at an age when settling down had been the last thing on her fun-loving mind.

'Fun-loving' was hardly the term to describe the mother Hayley knew. Her mum had spent the rest of her life resenting her forced marriage and the man she'd experimented with but hadn't been in love with. That pregnancy had resulted in Hayley's older sister, Laura, who had shouldered the burden of being the reason for her mother's unhappiness and her father's long-suffering misery. Hayley had decided she would not have sex until she was married to a man where an unexpected pregnancy would be welcomed. Because, with the best will in the world, contraceptives could fail, as they had for her and Cristos.

Now she paused on the threshold of the breakfast area, arrested by the sight of him sitting alone, dark head bowed over a laptop, a coffee cup shoved to one side. She had no doubt it was a self-imposed exile from the rest of the guests enjoying breakfast. Cristos would only be by himself from choice. Yet he seemed so alone.

Her heart turned over at the sight. After she'd left she'd been so intent on hating him she hadn't given much thought to how he'd been handling the split. Yet he'd never given up on her. She hadn't realised the efforts he'd put into finding her—thanks to the protective barrier put around her by her parents. For a long time she'd thought he'd abandoned her. When her parents had finally admitted they had shielded her from him, she'd established a life on her own. Had been, she re-alised, too scared to see Cristos again until she'd got herself completely together.

She had a sudden impulse to creep up behind him, wrap her arms around him and plant a kiss on the back of his neck as she'd often done. Then he would have pulled her into his lap, laughing and covering her face with kisses.

Instead she slid into the chair next to him. 'As you advised, I got through to the airline. My flight from Preveza is cancelled. Even if I could get to Lefkada, road transport to Athens wouldn't be a possibility. Apparently there's heavy snow all over the country and transport is in chaos.'

He closed his laptop. 'Then I guess you have to stop worrying and enjoy your bonus stay on Kosmimo.'

'I intend to,' she said. 'I texted my boss. Being stranded on a Greek island isn't a bad excuse for being late back to work. I feel like I've been let off school for a snow day.'

She leaned closer so only Cristos could hear. Felt her heart trip faster at the familiar scent of his skin. 'I'm sorry, Cristos. I know this isn't your fault that I'm stuck here. I've been most ungracious. Thank you for putting up with me.' On impulse, she kissed him on the cheek, closing her eyes for a brief second at the bliss of her lips on his smooth skin.

His eyes widened and she realised it was the first physical contact between them she had initiated. She pulled back to put more space between them.

'You're very easy to put up with,' he said with a slow lazy smile.

'Can I get you some breakfast?' she asked. 'Cake?'

When they'd visited Athens on their honeymoon she'd been amazed to find cake as a breakfast staple alongside the usual breakfast offerings at their hotel. Cakes like those she'd expect at morning or afternoon tea.

'None of that kind of cake at Pevezzo Athina. Remember, this is a holistic retreat style of resort. Here the cake is gluten free, dairy free and sugar free.'

Hayley wrinkled up her nose in dismay at the thought. He laughed. 'It's surprisingly good. You'll also find Greek yogurt, feta cheese, boiled eggs and fruit as well as some traditional Greek rusks that I think you might like. There's also a bar with lots of different teas.'

'And coffee, of course,' she said. Cristos had always loved his coffee, dark and thick.

'Only the best,' he said. 'I'm on my second. I've already eaten breakfast.'

Hayley glanced over at the buffet table. 'Alex and Dell have done very well to rustle up that kind of breakfast, considering the resort is closed and they weren't expecting all their guests to stay on.'

'They live on the island in the house Alex built on the next bay. No doubt they stocked up with the Australian visitors in mind. I don't know how long supplies will last if we're here for more than a few days though.'

'Surely the bad weather can't last that long. The reports I looked up said it was a freak snow-fall.'

'Who knows?' he said with an eloquent shrug of his shoulders. 'I hope for all our sakes it clears up. Everyone here is being positive about it but that won't last long.'

'Like you said, I intend to make the most of it.

With that in mind, I'd better go get some breakfast while the food lasts,' she said, only half in
jest.

As she got up from her chair the overhead lights
flickered, went dark, then came on again. There
was a collective, accompanying gasp from everyone in the room.

Cristos cursed. 'Losing power is just what we
don't need.'

Hayley's engineer brain went into action. The
company she worked for dealt mostly with large-
scale, industrial solar-power plants but they also
worked on smaller-scale projects like this one.
'There might be snow covering the solar panels.
And a slide of heavy, wet snow can break connections. What kind of battery storage do they
have here?'

'Enough for a few days, I assume,' he said.

'Diesel generator backup?' she asked, her mind
racing.

'Yes,' he said. 'Though they've never had to
use it.'

She thought for a moment. 'I've volunteered to
help clear up after breakfast. I think I could be

of more help with restoring the power. I'll go and see what I can do.'

Cristos picked up his laptop. 'I'll come with you.'

Cristos was lost in admiration of Hayley's knowledge and practical skills when it came to working with the island's power system. Fortunately, although there was a solid cover of snow, the wind had dropped so the low wind-chill factor made it possible for her to work outside.

She teamed up with one of the Athens cousins who was an electrician. Between them, Hayley and the cousin did their best to make sure the resort wasn't going to lose electricity. They fixed the faulty connection that had caused the power hiccup and got the generator ready to kick into action if required. There wasn't much for him and Alex to do except provide muscle where required.

It was a novelty for Cristos to take orders from his wife as she enlisted help to clear the snow from the panels. With a bunch of Greek men taking direction from a petite, blonde woman doing skilled manual work there was much good-natured banter. Cristos was surprised to see how well she took it, how happy and relaxed she seemed, giving as good as she got. He realised he knew nothing about her work in Australia, the life she had built up as an apparently single woman with no ring on her finger and no husband's name attached to hers.

And yet there had been no other man in her bed.

When it was done, he offered Hayley a hand to help her down the ladder, was surprised when she accepted. She'd been so keen to assert her independence.

'Thanks,' she said as she jumped the final step back onto the ground. This was the only time he'd been alone with her all morning.

'Careful, it's slippery there.' He put his arm around her to steady her. A helpful, impersonal touch, as even his grandfather might offer.

'Yes, we've churned up the snow and it's freezing into ice.'

She was wearing sturdy work boots provided by, surprisingly, his grandmother. Her work gloves had come from his grandfather. Stavros had helped wherever he could. Penelope had stood for a while observing the process before she'd disappeared back inside. Cristos detected a grudging admiration for Hayley from his *yia-yia*. His grandmother was a great believer in honest hard work—another of the reasons she'd loathed his father.

Once Hayley gained her balance she shrugged off his arm and rubbed both gloved hands together. 'A job well done,' she said with a sigh of satisfaction. 'We shouldn't have to worry about lighting or heating or access to the internet now. But we should try and keep the panels free of any further snowfalls.'

Her face was flushed high on her cheekbones, which accentuated the blue of her eyes and her naturally pink lips. It wasn't just cold, he realised, but exhilaration.

'You enjoyed that, didn't you?' he said.

'I did. I was glad to be able to help. It was interesting too, to see how things are done here with solar. There are some slight differences.'

'I can speak on behalf of everyone here when I say how grateful we are for your help.'

Hayley wore a bulky too-big jacket in an unflattering shade of brown and an even uglier fleece hat she'd found somewhere, her hair was dark with damp and clinging to her face, and her nose glowed red with cold. She looked beautiful.

'I thrive on hard work, Cristos. Always have.'

And he hadn't seen that. Or he'd seen it and glossed over it. He'd been so determined to give her the life his father had never given his mother that he had failed to see Hayley's needs—needs so very different from those of his mother from another generation and culture. He'd thought he knew what his wife needed—and hadn't listened to her when she'd told him what she wanted.

'It wasn't enough, was it?' he asked her now. 'The apartment in fashionable Brera in old Milan, the designer clothes we got at a discount, the parties.'

'I wasn't cut out to be a housewife, Cristos. Not at that age. Probably not at any age. The apartment was so tiny it took no time to clean. Brera was funky and fun but even shopping gets boring. Sitting at a café nibbling on *biscotti* and drinking the best *cappuccino* in the world paled after a while. If I didn't bury myself in a book, the Italian guys were annoyingly persistent in trying to pick me up. Remember, I didn't wear my wedding ring in public. I tried to learn the language but missed classes when you were back from a shoot so I could be with you. My friends had all finished uni and were working. The life of a kept woman wasn't really for me.'

'You tried to tell me all that—'

'But maybe not loudly enough. I didn't want to sound ungrateful. I mean… *Milano*. People would kill to live in such an exciting city.'

'But you were there too often on your own. I see that now.'

'Yes,' she said. The one word told him more than she might have imagined.

'And you thought I was with other women.'

'Sometimes. You're such a handsome man, I could see the hunger for you in their eyes.' Her voice trailed away.

'But not in my eyes,' he said. 'That was only for you.'

He'd had to handle unwanted attention from when he was a young teenager. Living in a tourist area meant women looking for a fling with a local. Someone to boast about after they'd gone home—like a sexual trophy. He'd even had older women suggesting they could initiate him. It had disgusted him. He'd only been interested in girls his own age. Good looks could be a burden, which was why he had been willing to try and earn money by exploiting them commercially— for him and Hayley. 'Do you believe me now that there was never any other woman?'

'Yes, I do,' she said firmly. 'Back then I doubted you because I was insecure. You were sometimes away for weeks at time. A man used to regular sex.'

'With his *wife*. I was trying to do the best I could for you, for *us*.' He couldn't keep the note of anguish from his voice, cursed himself for it. One thing that had been drilled into him was that a man never showed weakness. He couldn't let the mask slip.

'And I wanted to let you shine,' she said. 'I never wanted to squash my husband the way my mother did to my dad. Whatever you felt you needed to do, I was behind you. But while you shone, I… I grew duller and duller. Until I was so tarnished I felt you didn't see me any more.'

How could his beloved Hayley ever have got to feel that way? How had he taken his eye so off the ball? 'Never,' he said. 'You were never, *ever* dull in my eyes.' He looked down into her face.

'You have to believe that. You were smart, beautiful—still are—and all I wanted to do was give you a good life.'

'You came home with stories of shoots in Venice and I struggled to find something interesting to say about my day. I needed to work, to have a life outside that apartment.'

'We should have moved back to London.' He cursed. 'Why didn't I know you were feeling like that?'

'Why didn't I tell you? I look back and see I also was at fault when back then I thought it was only you in the wrong.'

He shook his head. 'You're being way too reasonable. Way too English. You shouldn't have had to tell me. I should have realised. And then when you got pregnant I—'

A switch seemed to turn off behind her eyes and she put up her hand in the thick glove. 'You know I don't want to talk about that. Especially not here, not now.' She looked over his shoulder and he turned.

Dell was headed their way with steaming mugs of coffee and his favourite cheese pie, *tiropita*. His cousin's wife, a food blogger, had become quite the Greek food aficionado since she'd married Alex.

'Hayley, you're a wonder woman,' Dell said. 'I can't believe you know how all that stuff works and how to fix it.'

Hayley shrugged but she looked pleased. 'It's my job,' she said. 'And I'm glad to be of help.'

'Seriously, we would have been in big trouble if we'd lost power. I really don't know how to thank you.'

Hayley, flushed with pleased embarrassment, looked up to Cristos for help with the answer.

'My wife is a wonder woman all right,' he said. He put his arm around Hayley to draw her close, though he could scarcely feel where her waist was through the jacket. 'And she's family, of course she wants to help.'

Dell smiled and Cristos could tell she was delighted that he and his estranged wife were getting on so well. He hoped he would never have to tell her the truth. Dreaded the thought of Hayley becoming part of family history as Cristos's English ex-wife.

Dell indicated the coffee and pie she held on a

tray. 'I've brought nourishment, but you should come inside.'

Hayley shook her head. 'I'd love a snack but I don't want to go inside. It's cold out here but so beautiful. Like a fairyland.' The clouds were clearing and a pale sun glinted off the snow reflecting like tiny crystals. They had woken up to a completely different, snow-shrouded landscape.

'I'll stay here with you,' he said, holding the tray for Dell. 'I've never seen the island under snow either.'

'None of us have,' said Dell. 'But it's too darn cold for my Aussie blood.'

Hayley took a piece of the pie—crisp filo pastry enclosing a savoury cheese filling—and a mug of coffee. 'Thanks Dell, it was worth getting up on that roof just to taste this.'

'Don't thank me,' said Dell. 'Thank Penelope. She baked the *tiropita* and she suggested I bring it out to you.' She smiled at Cristos. 'And you too, of course, Cristos. She said it's been your favourite since you were a little boy.'

Hayley's eyebrows rose. 'Did I hear that right? Penelope sent me out some pie?' She glanced up at Cristos.

'Looks like you're making a good impression,' he said. 'Who knew getting your hands dirty on a diesel generator would get you into *Yia-yia's* good books.'

He laughed, but inside he felt bleak. Maybe if Hayley had felt welcome in his family she might not have run so far away from him. But perhaps that had had more to do with her parents' dislike of him. Whatever had happened, he'd always had a feeling her mother had stage-managed it.

'What was that you said about making a snow-man on the beach?' he asked Hayley. 'When you've finished your pie, I'll take you down there.'

'I'd like that,' she said. 'I might even challenge you to a snowball fight.' Cristos tried not to think of tussling with Hayley in the snow, pinning her down, claiming a kiss because he won. Or conceding defeat and letting her have her way with him.

'Before you do,' said Dell, 'I'd like to run an idea by you. The troops are getting restless, not knowing when they're going to get off the island. Alex and I thought we might have a party tonight. What do you think?'

'I think it's a very good idea,' Cristos said.

'Me too,' said Hayley.

'It's Valentine's Day tomorrow,' said Dell. 'What do you think of a Valentine's theme? You two lovebirds should approve.'

Cristos sensed Hayley still and watched the colour drain from her face. How could Dell be so insensitive? But how could he blame her? He and Hayley had obviously put on too good an act of being reconciled.

He shrugged. 'Valentine's? Sure. Why not?'

'What about you, Hayley? You seem a bit stunned by the idea,' said Dell.

Cristos could see Hayley's struggle to compose herself. 'I was just wondering what people would wear. I've only got the trousers and sweater I wore yesterday and these jeans.'

'That's not a problem,' said Dell. 'I can loan you something. I'm a size bigger than you now but I've got smaller clothes I haven't been able to fit into since Georgios was born. The other guests are in the same boat clothes-wise but no one will really care. They all wore something nice for our vow-renewal ceremony—they can wear that again.'

'Okay,' said Hayley. 'I'll take you up on that offer. Thank you.'

She didn't meet his gaze. The word *'lovebirds'* hung between them as if it were really a bird, fluttering its wings for attention.

'It doesn't matter what people wear,' he said. 'It will keep people's minds off their plight and we'll all have fun.'

'What can I do to help?' asked Hayley.

'Nothing,' said Dell. 'You've done more than enough. All you have to do is enjoy yourself. Isn't that right, Cristos?'

Dell glanced back over her shoulder to give him a knowing look before she headed back into the resort with her tray.

CHAPTER TEN

HAYLEY DREADED THE Valentine-themed party. Not because she didn't think it was a good idea. As Dell had said, the guests were indeed getting fed up with their enforced vacations and wanting to get back to their homes. Tempers were fraying and annoyance being expressed, even with the awareness that the delay was no one's fault but Mother Nature's. Down on the beach that afternoon some of the snowballs had been thrown by the older kids with rather too much vigour and there'd been more than the odd tantrum from the toddlers. A party might help everyone relax.

No, that was not what bothered her about the party. The reason she was tying herself up in anxious knots was that she and Cristos were obviously expected to act like 'lovebirds'.

Getting to know Cristos again wasn't in any way straightforward. Being in such proximity to him was slowly scratching at the scars of old memories from their shared past. And then there were the scars beneath the scars. The painful process was forcing her to really look at her relationship with her husband and the circumstances that had ended it. And some of it puzzled her.

Then there was the shadow that the past threw on the present. She'd thought she was happy in Sydney. But seeing Cristos again was messing with her head—as well as sending all sorts of confusing messages to her body. Her job was fulfilling, she'd made new friends, she lived in a charming older-style apartment on the north shore near Sydney Harbour. What was missing was a man. *Her* man.

Could any man ever match up to Cristos?

Rather than bundling the past into a big box to shove somewhere in the recesses of her mind, with the divorce being the ribbon neatly tying it all up, she was beginning to rethink her time with Cristos.

Could she have got him wrong back then?

Trouble was, if she were Hayley and he were Cristos, Dell and Alex's guests having just met for the first time yesterday—she'd be madly attracted to him and excited at the possibility of falling for him.

As it was, she and Cristos were still wearing their wedding rings and she was more mixed up than ever. Would the evening involve more fake embraces and fake kisses? Each time she remembered how happy she'd been with him, she wanted those kisses to be real.

Cristos had not been back to 'their' room since he'd left that morning and it felt very empty without him. She closed her eyes to try to recapture his presence, his scent, but there was only the lemon and thyme tang of the resort shampoo she had just used in the shower. She looked over to that big, empty bed. Forced herself not to walk over to it. *Not* a good idea to go lie down on 'his' side, put her head on his pillow and try and breathe in his essence. Though she couldn't promise she wouldn't do that after the party when she climbed between those cold solitary sheets.

She wondered what his grandparents would make of Cristos bunking down on their sofa. Penelope would probably be delighted. And yet… Penelope was turning out to be not quite the witch Hayley had thought her. As evidenced by the gorgeous shoes Cristos's grandmother had loaned her for the evening.

She was going to the party in borrowed finery. Dell had rummaged through her wardrobe to find her a stylish dress in just the right size, elegant with a nod to retro. The fitted bodice with a scoop neck enhanced her curves and revealed a glimpse of cleavage; the tight, three-quarter-length sleeves were perfect for the cold weather, and the skirt was cut in a slim line with a split at the back. It made her wiggle when she walked.

'Perfect for Valentine's,' Dell had enthused. 'It really suits you.'

Trouble was, the dress was pink. And Hayley never wore pink. She'd always wanted to be taken seriously in her career in a man's world. Petite, blonde and dressed in pink just didn't cut it.

But to refuse Dell's kind offer would have been exceedingly impolite. 'Thank you, Dell,' she'd said as she'd hugged her new friend. 'It's a lovely dress.' Besides, it wasn't a bright candy pink, it was more a soft dusky rose. And looked way better on than she would have imagined. Maybe she should rethink pink.

But she only had knee-length daytime boots

with her. And Dell's shoes were too big to borrow. That was where Penelope, who had the same size feet as Hayley, had come to the rescue. She'd insisted Hayley borrow a pair of smart, pewter-coloured stilettos subtly adorned with anthracite-like beads across the pointed toes. 'I brought an extra pair with me for the ceremony,' Penelope had explained. They'd fitted perfectly and looked fabulous with the dress.

She'd just slipped into the shoes ready to go downstairs. She pointed her foot in front of her to better admire them. These were not old lady shoes. Hayley had lived in Milan long enough to recognise them as Italian designer. She had thanked Penelope with genuine delight.

But she'd fussed around with the dress and shoes long enough. Her hair and make-up were fine too. Luckily she'd had some basic make-up packed in her handbag—for a final touch up after the boat ride before she'd faced Cristos yesterday for the first time in so long.

Now it was time to head down to the party. If she was late, she would only draw attention to herself and she had no desire to be conspicuous. It was bad enough knowing she'd be entering a room where everyone knew each other and where they all were, in one way or the other, curious about her.

She picked up the small purse Dell had loaned her and click-clacked in the stilettos across the marble floor to the door. As she did so there was a knock on the door. Cristos.

'Are you decent?' he called as she slid open the security lock.

'If your definition of "decent" includes a pink frock, then I'm decent enough.' This was a game they'd used to play. The favoured answer had been: *No, I'm indecently naked and what are you going to do about it?* Hardly appropriate on this occasion. But how much fun their inappropriate, private times had been.

Hayley had to brace herself against the wall against a paralysing wave of sadness for all they'd lost. The fun—that was what had gone first. The love had dissipated more slowly.

Her heart kicked up a beat as she opened the door. Wearing black jeans and a black linen shirt, with his black hair and his jaw already shadowed, Cristos's dark-lashed eyes blazed green, the only colour in a gloriously dark image. He'd starred in a magazine campaign once where the page was printed in black and white, the exception being his extraordinary eyes. Here was the commercial come to life and she swooned over it.

She stared at him, unable to move, unable to say anything, overcome again by that yearning she was powerless to control. Never could she want another man the way she wanted him, had always wanted him.

It's just sex, it's just sex, she chanted to herself in time to the frantic thudding of her heart.

Did he guess?

He didn't say anything, just looked at her in return, that green gaze taking in her appearance from her hair—which she suspected he didn't like cut so short—right down to the tip of his grandmother's shoes. He used to look at her like that just before he was about to kiss her.

Her breath quickened and her lips parted as if of their own volition. *Yes!* But he stepped back and the moment was broken. She found her voice, forced it to stay steady. 'Did you come to check on me?'

'It would be expected that I escort my wife into the party,' he said.

'Of course,' she said.

'I've never seen you wear pink,' he said. 'It suits you, your skin, your eyes.' His voice broke, perhaps from the same effort she was making to ignore the sexual hum between them. 'You look beautiful. You have never been invisible to me. It's unbearable that you should ever have thought that true. Unbearable you should think it now.'

'I... I...' She didn't know what to say to him.

For a long moment, his gaze connected with hers and she could not look away. He reached out his hand to trace a line with his thumb from her cheekbone to the edge of her mouth. A wave of awareness swept over her, and she trembled beneath his touch.

He used to work such magic with his fingers.

'Th...thank you,' she managed to choke out.

He pushed his fingers through her hair and she closed her eyes for a moment at the bliss of it. 'Why did you cut it?'

'For a change,' she said.

Because he had loved it and she'd wanted in some way to spite him.

'When I got to Australia I wanted a new start, a new me. Also it gets very hot and humid in the summer in Sydney. It's more comfortable this short.'

'I like it,' he said.

'You do? I thought you would loathe it.'

'It was a shock, I admit. But it's cute and—'

'You know I don't like being called "cute",' she said with mock reprimand.

'If you'd let me finish, I was going to say it was cute and elegant at the same time. It suits you. So does the pink dress.'

'It's a nice dress, isn't it? Although it's not really my colour.'

'Maybe it should be. As I said, you look beautiful.'

'I'm glad you think so.'

He looked down. 'Are those my grandmother's shoes you're wearing? Surely not?'

'She loaned them to me.'

'Really? She has quite the shoe collection. A friend of hers owns an upscale shoe store and she gets them at a discount. I can't believe she loaned them to you. That's quite an honour.'

'I know. First the cheese pie and now Italian shoes. I'm wondering what's going on when I know she hates me.'

'She never really knew you.'

'You mean she never gave me a chance.'

'Maybe you've surprised her.' He shrugged. 'Whatever the reason, it was a long time ago. Right now I think my *yia-yia* is very impressed with you. I don't know, though, that she could actually come out and say it. Perhaps this is her way of letting you know that maybe she thinks we're not such a bad match after all.'

Her mouth twisted. 'Ironic, isn't it? Now that we're no longer a couple.'

Cristos put up his hand to stop her. 'Hayley, can we put aside all that for tonight? Let's forget our issues, forget why you're really here. Let's just enjoy this party. Have fun. You used to like parties and Alex and Dell throw a good one. Besides, the weather might lift in the morning and you'll be gone and we won't see each other again.'

It was what she wanted—or at least what she'd thought she'd wanted—but she felt as though his words had turned into frosty shards, like the icicles that hung from the windows, to pierce her heart.

'You mean we should celebrate the end of our marriage?'

His brow furrowed. 'I don't see it as something to celebrate. But since yesterday everything has been turned upside down and I don't know what's normal or not. If you like, you can call it our own private divorce party while the others are celebrating Valentine's.'

'That's awful. No. We can celebrate Valentine's too and remember—'

'How we were once happy, we once loved each other and we should celebrate the happy years while we mourn the end of them?'

'Okay. Yes. Good idea.' She thought it was a terrible idea. She wanted to cry rather than act as if she were having a ball.

'C'mon. I'm going to a party with a girl who looks delectable in a pink dress and my grandmother's shoes.'

'And I'm going with The Sexiest Man in Europe—'

He groaned. 'Can you please not call me that?'

'Who…who used to be my best friend.' Her voice trailed away.

He was silent for a long moment. 'And who will be your friend for one more night,' he said, his voice husky.

She forced a smile; if she didn't she would break down into sobs. 'Right. Let's get on with it, shall we?'

'It's party time.' He cleared his throat and she could see it was an effort for him to keep up the jolly pretence.

Why had they hurt each other so much?

'Is there anything you need from the room before we go?' she asked.

'No,' he said. 'I'll stay on my grandparents' sofa tonight.'

'You'd better remember to pretend to snore if you're going to go with the I-kicked-you-out-of-our-room story.'

'I'll do that,' he said, making a snoring noise that made her smile. Her smile turned into a smirk and he immediately picked up on it. 'What's that for?'

'If my own grandparents are anything to go by, it will be the old people doing the snoring. Hope you've got some earplugs.'

He rolled his eyes. 'Can we not even think about that?' He took her arm. 'Let's go or we'll be late. Are you ready?'

'I think so,' she said, drawing out the words, narrowing her eyes.

He gave a mock patient sigh she recognised of old. 'You're not going to turn back as soon as we get to the elevator because you suddenly remembered you need to go to the bathroom? Or want to fill your water bottle?'

She raised her eyebrows. 'Would I do that?'

'You know you would. Why do you think I came to get you five minutes earlier than I needed to? Just like I always did.'

Hayley laughed but her heart felt as if it were bleeding. Those private little rituals of a long-time couple. She'd forgotten how comfortable she had felt with them. She had always checked to see if he'd shaved properly; he'd often miss a little patch of those dark bristles on the underside of his chin. If she reached up to look now, to trail her fingers over his skin, she'd probably break down. Or maybe he'd managed so long without her he didn't need her to check for him.

The advantage of no one knowing her in Australia was they took her at face value. The disadvantage was that no one really knew her. But then no one had ever known her better than Cristos. Or so she'd thought.

'I'm not taking a water bottle to a party. But come to think of it, I do need to touch up my lipstick.'

He made a big exaggerated groan. 'Be quick, will you?' Just as he'd always said.

'Kidding,' she said. 'I just wanted to make you bite. Like you always did.'

He laughed. Then took her by surprise with a swift, hard kiss on her mouth. 'Now you do need to fix your lipstick but I'm not going to let you. C'mon, let's go party.'

For the last time.

CHAPTER ELEVEN

CRISTOS WANTED TO rip off the masks he felt obligated to wear and enjoy without pretence the company of his wife while he still had her by his side. But he was caught between two masks that were becoming increasingly suffocating.

To his family and friends, he presented a united front with the woman who had left him and had put him through the humiliating experience of not being able to find her. The masquerade of playing reconciling husband and wife had been his idea, intended only for the duration of Alex and Dell's celebrations. He had not anticipated the charade extending the way it had because of the extreme weather. The more Cristos and Hayley acted as husband and wife, the more his family and friends believed in it—and the more they welcomed her as part of the family. It would be awkward when she left.

The second, increasingly uncomfortable mask

was the one he wore when he was alone with Hayley. He could not reveal to anyone—least of all to her—that she still had immense power to wound him and how spending so much time with her was a constant stab to his heart.

She was different but still the Hayley he had signed up to for a lifetime of commitment. He'd agreed to a civilised, getting-to-know-each-other-again way to spend her enforced time on the island. In truth, what he wanted to do was find out what the hell had gone wrong, fix it and have her back where she belonged. With him. As his wife.

But she'd made it clear she didn't want that. Didn't want him to pressure her. He couldn't very well grab her and drag her back to his cave.

As soon as he walked into the party with his beautiful girl in her pink dress on his arm, Cristos felt the change in attitude towards Hayley from the gathered family and friends. There were more warm smiles and less curious glances. As Hayley had said, it was ironic that just as they were headed for divorce, his English wife was being embraced by her Greek in-laws.

Several people approached them with the express purpose of thanking Hayley for her work on ensuring the electricity supply to the resort. Hayley, in her usual modest way, demurred, explaining it was her job to know such things but thanking them with warmth.

He was so proud of her.

And yet that pride was mingled with pain that she'd had to leave him to achieve her own career. He had not nurtured her or encouraged independence while leaving her on her own. If he had his way, things would now be very different—he worked mainly from home and the face-to-face meetings he had were brief. But her heart was barricaded against him.

Hayley looked around her. 'Dell has done a fabulous job decorating the room. How did she conjure all this up?'

His cousin and his wife had rearranged the guest living room and dining area to allow an area for dancing. Big pink and red paper hearts and bunches of red and white balloons festooned the walls. The wealthy, sophisticated guests who usually frequented Prevezzo Athina would probably be horrified at its transformation into a Greek family party venue. What did Hayley call this kind of gathering? A knees-up. But the stranded guests were hooting their approval.

Valentine's Day had never been a big thing for Cristos. He'd celebrated it because Hayley had got a kick out of it. But to him Valentine's was for single people looking for love, not for couples who celebrated their love every day. Now all the references to romance just reminded him at every turn of what he'd lost. But she was here and, as he had reminded himself many times already, that was a much better situation than the two years and five months he'd spent without her.

'Dell has kids,' he said. 'She probably has all that craft stuff stashed at home. And remember Alex was the nightclub king of Sydney. He knows a thing or two about hosting a party.'

'They've done a great job, especially considering the circumstances.'

He agreed. To have got all this together at such short notice was impressive. There was a barman serving pink and red romance-themed cocktails with names like Love Bite and Kiss on the Lips, as well as champagne. A young DJ with a hipster beard, who was the boyfriend of someone's niece, was in charge of the music. Heart-shaped hors d'oeuvres were circulating on trays to a roomful of guests determined to have a good time.

Including Cristos.

He was just about to suggest to Hayley that they dance when his grandmother came over to greet them. She was not, he was relieved to see, accompanied by the ever-present Arianna. He was not in the slightest bit interested in hooking up with his childhood friend. He'd thought it was incredibly bad form of Arianna to ogle him in the presence of his wife, with the implicit approval of his grandmother, and he'd done his best to avoid her.

But tonight Penelope's attention had switched to Hayley. She stood back at arm's length and critically surveyed his wife's outfit, finally giving it the thumbs up. 'Very nice,' she said.

'I'm grateful to Dell for the dress. But it's the shoes that make it, don't you think?' said Hayley. Bravo to his wife, who had no cause to like Penelope, for playing along with her game.

'I think so too,' said Penelope, preening at the compliment to her taste.

Hayley pointed her foot out in front of her. 'These shoes make me feel like Cinderella.' With his *yia-yia* as the fairy godmother? Cristos supposed stranger things had happened.

'You must have them,' Penelope said immediately. 'To keep, I mean.'

'Really?' said Hayley with genuine surprise. 'But I couldn't—'

His grandmother threw out her hands in a dismissive gesture. 'I have bunions that make these narrow shoes uncomfortable. I've only worn them once. They are yours now.'

'Are you sure?' Hayley asked. 'They're designer shoes and—'

Cristos nudged her. 'Thank you, *Yia-yia*. It's very kind of you,' he said. He nudged Hayley again.

Hayley leaned across and kissed Penelope on each cheek. '*Efcharisto poli*—thank you very much *Pentherl* Penelope.'

Penelope laughed. 'You called me your mother-in-law when I am your grandmother-in-law.'

Hayley flushed. 'I stand corrected.'

'It's no matter,' Penelope said. Her eyes clouded. 'I have been mother to Cristos since he was fourteen years old so you can think of me as your mother-in-law. I would like that. Or you can call me *Yia-yia*.'

After Penelope left them Cristos rolled his eyes. 'I think the unthinkable has happened. The matchmaker has reversed her decision—it will never be official, of course, but you've won her over, Hayley.'

'How?'

'By being your own sweet self. By pitching in and helping whenever you had the opportunity. Finally, she has respected my choice of bride.'

'Which isn't really valid any more, is it?' she whispered. 'She'll hate me more than ever when I leave.'

'I doubt that. Besides, you won't be here to worry about it.'

'But you will,' she said.

Worrying about his grandmother's reaction would be the least of his problems when he had to say goodbye for the last time to the wife he still wanted. But he didn't let his mask slip and let her know how he really felt.

It wasn't just Cristos's grandmother who welcomed her, the whole family embraced her and

Hayley was surprised how good it felt. Thank heaven she'd made an effort to learn Greek when she'd first met Cristos. Her language skills were rudimentary at best but people seemed delighted she'd made the effort. Then proceeded to chat in what was usually excellent English.

The only exception was a brief and rather unpleasant encounter with the woman who had been staring so lustfully at Cristos the day before when they were told about the storm. Thankfully Dell had seen what was happening and come over to rescue her.

Hayley told Dell about Penelope's gift of the shoes. 'That was nice of her. I'm so pleased you're getting on well with Penelope. She's a real friend to me, was wonderful from the word go. Wait until you and Cristos start a family—you'll never have to worry about a babysitter.'

Hayley tried to smile but she knew it came out as a poor imitation. She couldn't bear to think about babies and Cristos in the same thought. Dell misinterpreted her expression. 'Sorry. Silly of me. Of course you won't be living here. I guess you'll live in Cristos's apartment in Athens? Or maybe London?'

'We…er…haven't really got that far yet.'

'Of course, he could move to Sydney to be with you. I hope not. I mean, not that I don't love Sydney. It's home. But it's too far away from us here. I hope you stay in Europe. You know I love Cristos to pieces—as a cousin, of course—and I think you and I are friends already.'

'Of course, we are,' said Hayley. She'd liked Dell immediately.

'Keep that in mind, won't you?' said Dell. 'About us being friends, I mean.' She hugged her and Hayley hugged her back with genuine feeling.

'I most certainly will,' she said. 'And thanks again for the dress.'

'You're welcome,' said Dell. 'Please keep it. Now I've seen how great you look in it, I probably won't wear it again.' She patted her hips. 'By the time I shift this baby weight the dress will be out of fashion. Besides, I can't be outdone by Penelope, much as I love her.'

'You're too generous,' Hayley said, touched almost to tears. 'I love the dress. Thank you.' This particular shade of pink was growing on her.

'Think of your friend Dell when you wear it and I'll be happy.'

Hayley hugged her again. 'I see Alex beckoning you,' she said, looking over Dell's shoulder.

'He wants to dance. Alex was such a party boy before we met. I had to have dance lessons to keep up with him.'

Dell headed off to her husband. He swung her up in his arms and Dell laughed. Their love and joy in each other shone from them. When did that joy start to fade from her love for Cristos?

What would it take to fan it back to life?

The music switched to a Latin beat and within minutes Dell and Alex were dancing the salsa, dipping and twirling and undulating to the infectious beat. Hayley's feet started to tap and her body to sway.

'They look good, but are they as good as we were?' Cristos's voice came from behind her.

'I very much doubt it,' she said. 'We were the best.'

At Durham, she'd dragged him along to salsa-dancing classes not long after they'd met. He'd turned out to have amazing rhythm and style and had been very soon by far the best male dancer in the class.

Now he handed her a cocktail, a very pink

cocktail speared with a red cherry on a tooth-pick. 'The mixologist behind the bar—'

'The *what*?'

'That's what he called himself. He offered me a Lady in Red. I asked him to make me a Lady in Pink, just for you.'

'How gallant.' She sipped at the frothy pink confection. 'Very nice, and packs quite a punch. What are you drinking?' She eyed his red cock-tail.

'A pomegranate martini, using pomegranates grown on the island.'

'Very Greek,' she said. 'It looks good.' In the old days, she would have leaned forward without hesitation for a sip to taste.

'He told me to come back for a Kiss on the Lips.' Hayley raised her eyebrows. 'For you,' he hastily explained. 'The drink would be for you.'

She laughed. 'I dare not ask what comes next in that sequence. Perhaps a Screaming Orga—'

Now, why had she said that?

He grinned. 'This is a family party. He did mention he had some Hanky-Panky on offer.'

Hayley spluttered on her drink. 'We might leave it at that,' she said, laughing. 'Please don't abandon me for too long when you get me my Kiss on the Lips. Dell had to rescue me from your friend Arianna.'

He frowned. 'She's really not a friend of mine. Our grandmothers were friends and as kids we got thrown together, whether I liked it or not.'

'She actually isn't very nice, you know.'

He groaned. 'Tell me something I don't know. Even as a kid she had a hard edge to her. Hence the one ill-advised date.'

'You must have given her hope of some kind. She asked me had I left you because you were gay or did you leave me because I wasn't woman enough for you.'

Now it was Cristos's turn to splutter into his drink. He cursed in Greek. 'What did you say? I would have—'

'I can't remember the exact words but I think she got the message that it was none of her business.'

'Where is she now?'

'Diagonal corner, glaring at us. I think she's had quite a bit to drink.'

'She can't speak to you like that,' he said grimly. 'I'm going to—'

Hayley had always loved it when Cristos went all super-protective on her. But a confrontation with his unwanted admirer, who also happened to be a family friend, might not be the best idea. Something needed to be done to defuse the situation.

She put down her cocktail. 'Maybe a kiss on the lips might be a good idea right now.'

'But you haven't finished your—'

She looked up at him. 'I meant a real kiss on the lips, not the cocktail. You know, to show her that it was for neither of those reasons we split.'

Cristos stared at her for a long moment, disbelief in his eyes, then a slow smile spread across his face. 'With the greatest of pleasure,' he said.

She'd spoken more in jest but suddenly Hayley wanted Cristos to kiss her for real. No pretence. No hidden agenda. Just Cristos kissing her as he had so many times before. She wound her arms around his neck, tilted her head back in invitation. 'C'mon, kiss on the lips.'

His lips brushed hers gently at first, then with more pressure, his mouth firm and warm. She kissed him back with an enthusiasm that wasn't in the slightest bit staged. 'More,' she murmured against his mouth. 'We're lovebirds, remember.'

He needed no further urging and he claimed her mouth in a full-on passionate kiss, the tip of his tongue teasing hers. His kiss felt familiar, yet thrillingly new and she relaxed into the pleasure of it.

The public kiss, staged for the benefit of a mean-spirited woman who showed no respect for a man's wedding band, should have been enough but Hayley's body urged more. She wanted tongues and teeth and moans and sighs and that delicious shiver of want rippling through her body that a kiss from Cristos could always evoke. She wanted more than his kiss; she ached for the pleasure of his touch on her body, his hands running down the sides of her breasts. She wanted—

But they were at a family party on full display in front of his grandparents, cousins, friends and a number of kids. They couldn't continue this for longer than would constitute appropriate under such circumstances—even for a married couple.

But it was long enough and passionate enough to bring all the old feelings rushing back. And she kissed him back wholeheartedly and without reserve.

Finally he murmured against her mouth. 'That should do the trick.' But by then she scarcely remembered the original purpose of the kiss. She just wanted more. Perhaps it was the Lady in Pink loosening her inhibitions. Perhaps it was the build-up of tension between her and Cristos since she'd first sighted him on the clifftop outside the chapel. The unacknowledged desire that had never gone away. She strained against him, breast to chest, thigh to thigh, but even through the fog of want and unanswered questions common sense prevailed.

'Yes,' she said breathlessly, pulling away from him. She looked around him to where she'd last seen the woman who had given her a most unpleasant few moments. 'She's turned her back on us and is walking away.'

'I think that's the last trouble you'll get from her,' he said.

'As long as she doesn't trouble you after...after I go.'

He put his fingers on her lips to stop her. 'Didn't

I ask you not to talk about that? Tonight, it's just us partying and enjoying ourselves.'

'Sure,' she murmured. He obviously hadn't been as affected by the kiss as she had, although she noticed he was having to control his breathing. What could she do to let him know she wanted more, wanted *him*?

He took her hand, tugged her towards him. 'Come and dance with me. Ever since I saw Alex and Dell burning up the floor I've had a strangely competitive urge to show them what we can do. Are you with me?'

She took a deep breath to try and gather her thoughts, still her racing heart. 'Oh, yes. May the best couple win. And may that couple be us.'

'That's my girl,' he said.

They stood facing each other, waiting for the beat to start. Hayley felt a ripple of nerves. They'd danced so many times together in the past— would it be the same?

He swung her into the salsa. Immediately they found their rhythm. Salsa was fast, energetic, sensual with lots of hip swaying and turning, improvised lifts and shoulder shimmies. Their dance teacher had told them it had roots in Latin dancing like mambo and cha-cha but was also influenced by Afro-Caribbean rhythms. Hayley had done ballet and jazz for years and enjoyed them but it wasn't until she'd joined the dance club at uni that she'd got into salsa and loved it. But she'd never had a partner like Cristos. He was a superb dancer and she knew she was good too. Together they'd been sensational.

He'd started classes with her at Durham before they were married. Latin dance was sensual and passionate; dancing with him had been like extended foreplay, fully clothed. But she'd been determined to wait to make love until after they were husband and wife. She had wanted him so desperately, and he her, that she sometimes wondered if they'd got married young simply so they could have sex. But she dismissed the thought. How could she separate the lust and love and sheer enjoyment of a man's company? It had always been more than lust between them.

Back then they'd been perfectly matched as dancing partners. Now they slipped right into the steps as though it had been days rather than years since they'd danced together. She'd prefer a dress that wasn't as tight, and dancing shoes, but the tighter skirt gave more sway to her hips and she managed just fine. Cristos all in black was sensational; she found herself gasping at how sexy he was when he danced, how utterly beautiful. They were so in tune when they danced. As they had been in bed.

What would it be like to make love with her husband again?

They danced alongside Dell and Alex. 'Are you challenging us to a dance-off?' Alex called to his cousin. 'If so, bring it on.'

The two men threw their partners into ever more complex moves. Soon the other dancers had melted away from the dance floor as the two couples danced. Alex and Dell were good, very good. But Hayley thought Cristos was the superior male dancer and she was a trained dancer so that gave them an advantage. The observers cheering them on from the sidelines seemed to give them louder cheers but Alex and Dell were beloved and it was, after all, their party.

The dance-off was ultimately declared a draw, which was the only possible result. 'Although we really were the better dancers,' her competitive husband whispered in her ear.

Hayley could barely answer him. Dancing with Cristos had the same effect on her it always had. She felt flushed, exhilarated, breathless and more turned on than she would admit to from being held against his hard, strong body, pulsing her hips against his, feigning looks of passion that were anything but feigned. Excited because she realised his looks weren't feigned either.

But then she was whirled across to partner Alex while Cristos danced with Dell for a final salsa. The music switched to something more sedate and she found herself dancing in turn with the architect cousin from Athens, Alex's doctor father from Sydney, and finally her grandfather-in-law, Stavros, who tested her on the Greek he had taught her while they'd been packing away the outdoor furniture before the storm. She found she enjoyed the big Greek family celebration more than she would ever have imagined.

There was a short break for refreshments when the DJ switched to traditional Greek music. 'Are the men going to dance?' she asked Cristos, now back by her side.

He nodded. 'The men in our family enjoy *horos*.

The traditional dances of these islands are always part of our celebrations.'

'And the women? Do they dance too?'

'Of course. But not tonight.'

'Will you wear traditional costume?'

'At other parties, yes. But this is an impromptu party. No one would have come prepared.'

'Shame. I would have liked to see you in it.'

When the men started dancing to the infectious music, Hayley couldn't keep her eyes off Cristos. His natural rhythm and grace made even the simplest of steps look accomplished.

Dell was beside her, her eyes on her beloved Alex. 'They say some of these traditional dances started way back when as an innocuous way to flirt with women,' she said.

'I can see that,' Hayley replied, mesmerised by the sight of her husband as he dipped and swayed and turned in step with the other men in the traditional dances, laughing, happy, relaxed. She'd been kidding herself the whole time she'd been in Australia that she could forget him. And it had been a battle with herself to channel her thoughts towards divorce since the moment she'd first seen him again at the chapel. It wasn't that she was falling in love with him all over again.

She had never stopped loving him.

Finally the dancing ended and the guests started to dissipate and head to their rooms. Hayley stood about, uncertain of what to do next. Cristos had stated in no uncertain terms that he would not be sharing a room with her tonight. Yet they needed to keep up a pretence of unity.

Cristos was talking with an older man she had scarcely spoken to. She walked up to her husband, planted a kiss on his cheek and said she was going up to their room and she'd see him when he came up. It was a typical husband-and-wife exchange, words only meant to maintain the illusion of their marriage, and she thought she handled it well. But it took a real effort to keep her voice steady and light when she really wanted to beg him to come to her bed.

When she got there, she moped around the empty room. Her footsteps echoed on the marble floor, emphasising her aloneness. It was quiet outside and still. No new snow had fallen since dinner time. There was a chance this might be her last night on the island. She felt immeasurably sad at the thought of the divorce papers still packed away in her handbag.

She showered and changed into her pyjamas. They were very nice pyjamas and had cost an extraordinary number of euros. But she wouldn't take them back with her to Sydney. Wearing them would only evoke unwanted memories of her time on Kosmimo.

Thankfully her life in Sydney was so different it held no memories of Cristos. She would be able to put this episode behind her as if it were some kind of dream. Scratch that. Not dream. Nightmare. Because she had a niggling feeling that this night—the party, the kiss, the dancing—had been the last chance to put things right with Cristos.

She was brushing her teeth when she heard the knock on her door. At this time of night she thought she must have imagined it. But it came again.

Without thinking twice, she opened the door. There was no stranger danger here. But that was no stranger standing there. *Sheepish* wasn't ever a word she would have applied to her six-foot-two dark-haired Greek god of a husband. But that was the word that immediately sprung to mind.

'Cristos. Aren't you meant to be with your grandparents?'

He shrugged. And behind the sheepishness she could see a hint of devilment in his green eyes. 'They kicked me out. No sofa for this bad grandson tonight. Stavros told me to get upstairs and fix whatever I did wrong to my lovely wife.'

CHAPTER TWELVE

COULD SHE HAVE a one-night stand with her hot husband? With hungry eyes, Hayley drank in the sight of Cristos as he stood at the threshold of her room, his broad shoulders and powerful body framed by the doorway. She wanted him so much she felt giddy.

He looked vaguely dishevelled in the sexiest possible way, his jaw darkly shadowed, his eyes hooded, his mouth in a half-smile. The fact he looked uncertain of his reception made him seem even more appealing. Desire for him rippled through her.

The only man she had ever wanted.

She wanted to grab him and haul him to the bed. Or to the sofa or the rug or even up against the wall. They'd made deliriously exciting love in all those places.

Just one more time with him.

'Come in,' she said, her voice tight with pent-up longing. *Now.*

Her husband stepped across the threshold. She kicked the door shut behind him. 'But you're not sleeping on this sofa either,' she said.

His dark eyebrows rose. But she didn't give him an opportunity to question her. Instead she wound her arms around his neck and looked up at him with what she hoped he would recognise as blatant invitation. 'You're in the bed with me. And not with a row of pillows or any other barrier between us.' She suffered a momentary loss of bravado. 'Er…that is, if you want to be with me.'

His eyes narrowed in the way she had always found unbearably sexy. 'I never stopped wanting you, *koukla.*' His voice was deep and husky and she thrilled to his words.

He dipped his head and kissed her. In her bare feet she had to stretch up on tiptoe to meet his mouth with hers. She surrendered with a sigh to the bliss of his tongue stroking the seam of her lips, of her tongue welcoming his. *At last a proper kiss.* Not the fake, for-show kind that had been so deeply disturbing and unsatisfying. The kind of kiss with Cristos she remembered, so familiar yet so new and different.

How she had missed him.

So many kisses given and received over several years of marriage. There was the sweet, triumphant kiss of commitment on their wedding day; the quick friendly kiss to let her know he was home; the comforting kiss when something had gone wrong and a kiss was just the thing to help; and then the kiss like this one. A kiss of hunger unleashed, of rapidly rising passion, a no-going-back kiss that was the prelude to the kind of lovemaking that would have her almost fainting with pleasure—both the taking of it and the giving of it.

She clung to him, weak with excitement and arousal as her tongue answered his, as she pressed her body close to his, breasts to solid male chest, hips to the hardness of his thighs. Her murmurs of pleasure were answered by more pressure, more urgency, his groan of impatience. His hands slid down her shoulders to tear open her pyjama top, the buttons bouncing on the marble floor. At last he cupped her breasts, stroking and playing with her nipples, already erect and aching for his touch.

It felt so good.

She slid her hands down his back to tug his shirt free from his trousers, slid them up to caress his back, smooth skin over rippling muscles.

At last.

She didn't have to haul him to the bed. He picked her up as if she weighed nothing and carried her there, breaking the kiss only for as long as it took to place her down then join her. He slid the silky pyjama top over her shoulders and down her arms until it lay next to her and her breasts were bared. She raised her hips to help him tug her pyjama pants down and toss them on the floor.

'I liked my lady in pink,' he murmured, his eyes narrowed and intent as he stroked the length of her body, first with his eyes then with his large, warm hands. 'But I so prefer my lady in nothing.'

'Two can play at that,' she said, laughing, as she fumbled with the buttons of his shirt, quickly rid him of his clothes. Then there was no more talk, just a slow burn of moans and sighs as they explored each other and made up for lost time.

* * *

Cristos had fallen into the deep sleep of a sexually satisfied, contented man. Contented because he had made love with the wife who had been missing from his life for so long, but whom he had never stopped wanting. Satisfied because they had lost count of the times they had brought each other to the ultimate peaks of pleasure.

The early-morning light filtering through the shutters woke him. For that split second between sleep and awareness he wasn't sure where he was. Then he remembered and a great surge of exultation had him wide awake. *Hayley.* This was not one of the many dreams of her that had haunted him for so long. She was real.

His wife lay beside him, her head nestled against his shoulder, one arm flung across his chest, one leg entwined with his. Her cheeks were flushed, her mouth swollen to a pout from his kisses. In places her tender skin was reddened with beard rash. He felt not a jot of regret. He had been tender with her but they had kissed and made love with mutual enthusiasm. His beard had left its mark on her and not just on her face—he had kissed her all over. He was glad he had marked her. *She was his.*

Her fine, short hair was tousled and he gently smoothed it back into place with his hand. He breathed in the intoxicating scent of her, of *them*. Risked dropping a gentle kiss on her temple.

She stirred. Cristos held his breath. He wanted to prolong this quiet moment of union. Just he and Hayley together as they should be, husband and wife. Because he knew it couldn't last. Making love hadn't solved their problems. Might even have caused more.

He didn't want this to be the end of it for him and Hayley. A night together for old times' sake and then they both moved on. If she went back to Sydney—perhaps tomorrow, maybe even as soon as today—he wanted to go with her. He never wanted to let her go.

However, if there were to be any chance of moving forward together, they had to revisit the past. And he did not imagine it would be anything other than a painful journey. For each of them. But he had to know the truth about why she had left him and made it impossible for him to find her. In turn, he had to strip himself of the masks he had variously worn and present his real face to her. To right the wrongs he had done her.

After that, he hoped they could find their way back to each other. He imagined a renewal-of-vows ceremony like the one Alex and Dell had just taken part in. Perhaps a service where the church blessed their union as his traditional grandparents had so wished.

Or not.

Cristos didn't want to think about the *or not* option. He did not want to give up on Hayley. He wanted to right the wrongs of the past and have his wife back by his side. This time for the rest of their lives. The thought of growing old with her made him smile—she would be a cute, feisty old lady—and he longed for it to happen so desperately he found himself praying for the first time in many years.

His leg was starting to go numb from the pressure—light though it was—of her leg over his when finally Hayley stirred. Her eyes fluttered open, looked uncertain for a moment then widened when she realised where she was. The first expression was happiness, joy even, and as she reached out for his hand they shone a brighter shade of blue. But the joy was quickly suffused with panic and she started to edge away from him. He held her hand firm.

'Before you try to scoot away from me and go back to being ice princess Hayley, you need to tell just why you left me nearly two and a half years ago.'

She bit down on her lower lip. 'You know, I've told you—'

'Not all of it. There are gaps in your story, *koukla*. Gaps I've puzzled over how to fill for too long.'

He pulled her close to him, loving the slide of her nakedness against his. His arm secured her close to him.

'You know all you need to know.'

Her voice quivered and he knew she wasn't telling him the truth. *Why?* He thought he'd gone through every possible scenario in his mind but had never reached a viable conclusion.

'No, I don't know,' he said. 'Those last weeks, those last days, you need to fill me in. There are also things I have not told you about me that you might want to hear.'

He felt her stiffen beside him. 'Such as?'

'Things about myself I felt…ashamed to tell you.'

'What do you mean?' She twisted so she lay on her side and her eyes met his. 'I've often felt that I don't really know you. That perhaps I never really knew you at all.'

Those blue eyes saw through him, realised the masks were there. She was, perhaps, the only person who had ever sensed there was someone different underneath.

'I always thought I knew you,' he said, not intending tit-for-tat, just telling it the way he saw it. 'It was a shock to realise I didn't. I had not imagined the Hayley I loved could be so callous.'

She gasped. 'That's very harsh.'

'That's how it felt. Complete indifference on your part to my feelings, to our marriage. Not to mention I was worried sick about you. I had questions about why you left but could never find answers—because I couldn't find you. Of course, me being away that night and leaving you alone was unforgivable. You know I will never forgive myself.'

He didn't expect her to contradict him. She nodded mutely in acknowledgment and again his anger at himself burned through him. But he would have been there afterwards for her—if he'd been given the chance.

'Losing our baby was tragic,' he said. 'With you thirteen weeks pregnant, us becoming parents was beginning to feel real. Something I really wanted. I mourned the loss too, although I never got the chance to cry with you. But other couples survive a miscarriage and go on to try again. I know you blame me for not being there—and I was at fault, more at fault than you guessed—'

Her eyes narrowed. 'So there was something—'

He gently laid his finger over her mouth. 'Let me speak, *koukla*. You never gave me the chance to speak with you about that night that tore our marriage apart. Then you ran away from me. Can you imagine how worried I was? How frantic to find you?' How like a piece of dirt on her shoe his mother had made him feel when he had arrived on their doorstep in Surrey looking for his wife.

Hayley turned away so he couldn't see her face

and her voice was muffled by the pillow. She might have said she was sorry but he couldn't be sure. He put his hand on her bare shoulder, warm and soft. He never wanted to lose her again. But something poisonous had happened that night and it had festered. There could be no hope for a genuine reconciliation unless it was lanced.

Hayley turned to face him again. All colour had drained from her face. 'I only realised in these last days what it must have been like for you. I had convinced myself I hated you. My family— my parents and my sister—never told me how hard you'd tried to find me. It hurt that you'd let me go so easily.'

'I assure you I did everything in my power to find you. I had lost my world. Not just the child I wanted so much, but you. The wife I adored.'

'Why did my parents—?'

'I think we know the answer to that,' he said. There had been a distinct note of triumph in her mother's voice at their last encounter. But he had not given up.

'I didn't know. But at first I wouldn't have cared if you were hurting. In truth, I wanted you to hurt. After a while I convinced myself you were off with another woman. Probably Ginny. Living happily ever after with a tall, long-legged model.'

To hear such bitter words spoken, not with venom but with sadness, was devastating to him. 'I can't believe you thought that,' he said. 'That you ever thought I wanted anyone but you. From the moment I saw you in that pub in Durham there was only ever you.'

He turned her so that she was forced to face him. She sat up, blushed, clutched the sheets to cover her nudity. She *blushed*. After all the ways he'd made love to her and she to him over the last hours, and she blushed. He found it delightful.

'I have to go to the bathroom,' she said.

For one hideous moment he thought she would go into the bathroom and not come back. She would somehow escape and find her way out of the resort and onto a waiting boat and he would never see her again. He gritted his teeth to restore sanity to his thoughts. There was no trapdoor in the bathroom, no secret network of tunnels under the building. It was just his imagination running crazy, as it had when he'd feared something was wrong with her.

Until first her sister and then her mother had

told him Hayley was alive and well but just didn't want to see him. He had thought he'd heard her mother mutter, *Can't you get that into your thick Greek head?* But perhaps that had been an echo of his own thoughts. Many times he had berated himself for continuing the search for a woman who didn't want him.

Now he watched as she made a dash for the bathroom. Her back view was as beautiful as her front, slender with a narrow waist and curving hips too wide to make her a model but just right for a sensuous woman who was everything he'd ever wanted. He loved the new way her hair feathered to the nape of her neck, soft and fine. He had enjoyed kissing her there.

She came back with a white hotel towel wrapped around her from her chest to her thighs. He was sad as he could never have enough of admiring her body. But perhaps it was for the best as he would only want to make love to her again and there were things that had to be said. He pulled the sheet over himself and sat up straight.

'We need to talk,' he said. He'd always found that an ominous set of words when someone said it to him. But in this case it was true. He was no closer to understanding what had gone wrong.

She carried two glasses of water and handed him one without speaking. They'd always joked that making love was thirsty work. He wanted that ease between them back. He wanted the laughter. Most of all he wanted the love. He had never stopped loving her. He had to give his everything to this last-ditch effort to mend things between them.

Hayley sat on the edge of the bed next to him, modestly tugging the towel into place. He felt at a disadvantage reclining against the pillows and sat up so they could face each other as equals.

'Why were you so concerned about Ginny?' he said. He wished he'd never met the woman—although he wouldn't have made so much money so quickly without her.

'We seemed to bump into her more than could be put down to coincidence within the circles we moved in. I could see she wanted you, and she was the kind of woman who dismissed me with indifference. As if I were beneath her tall, skinny attention. Even though she believed I was your girlfriend, if not your wife.'

'I didn't know that,' he said.

'Why would you?' she said. 'What was she to you?'

'I was doing business with her.'

Hayley took a sharp intake of breath. 'So, I wasn't wrong that there was something going on between you two.'

He put up his hand. 'Strictly business.'

He hadn't realised until he was well into the deal how predatory Ginny was. How at one stage she'd intimated that *he* was part of the bargain. He had quickly disillusioned her about that—he loved his girlfriend, he'd told her, choking on the lie 'girlfriend' when he'd proudly wanted to proclaim Hayley as his wife.

'What kind of business?'

'She and her brother are both very smart people. They were developing a shopping comparison app. I invested in it. It was a brilliant concept, just right for the time.'

She frowned. 'You didn't tell me.'

'I didn't want to concern you.'

'That's rubbish. Surely any business deal you were doing was my concern. We were married. And I thought we shared everything.'

This was it. The make it or break it. The kicker that might cause her to walk right out of the room and his life. No need for escape routes through the bathroom. 'I didn't want you to know I was a gambler. And I had put a considerable chunk of our savings at risk.'

He couldn't meet her eyes, dreading what he might see there.

CHAPTER THIRTEEN

HAYLEY STARED AT CRISTOS, unable to comprehend what she was hearing. 'What do you mean?' Her husband, now her lover again, was suddenly a stranger to her. Even though he lay naked in her bed. Cristos a gambler?

What else had he been hiding from her?

She swallowed hard against her disbelief and disappointment. 'What was it? Horses? Casino? Online gaming?'

He shook his head. 'Not that kind of gambling. I told you about my trading stocks and shares at university, backing the small apps my fellow students were developing. Once I started to earn big money with modelling, I upped the stakes and took that a step further. Investing a lot more money in untried businesses where I saw potential. With a lot more risk.'

Hayley frowned. 'I'm not sure what you're getting at. Are you talking something dishonest?'

Fear grabbed at her with icy claws. Cristos a criminal? She couldn't bear the thought. 'Something illegal?'

He shook his head. 'I'm talking one hundred per cent legitimate investment. But not of the blue-chip kind—think the total opposite of blue-chip investment. Where the risks are so much higher.' There was an edge of excitement to his voice.

'You sound as though you enjoyed it.'

'I did. I do. When the odds are stacked against you, when it's a bigger leap of faith than you thought yourself capable of, when there's a very real risk you could lose everything on something as intangible as an idea to be thrown out into cyberspace—there's something heart-stopping about it. That's the kind of gambling I risked our savings on.'

The feeling that she had never known this man intensified. 'How? I would have known. We had a joint bank account.'

'Confession time,' he said, his green eyes sober. She steeled herself for his answer. 'I still had my own account. I diverted some of my earnings into it. You never saw them. That was my seed money.'

'But you were earning so much.' More money than two young people could have dreamed of at that time.

'More than you knew.'

She clutched at her heart. 'I can't believe you did that. Why didn't you tell me?'

'Two reasons. The first was that I was ashamed to be a gambler. I was doing it for our future. But I didn't want to look diminished in your eyes. Be someone less than you thought me.'

'Less? Why would you think that? My father is a banker. He used to say that the money market was just one big gambling den. Trading on currency, trading on futures, on the price of commodities. Not the kind of desperate gambling that's an addiction, an illness, that ruins people's lives. That wasn't you, was it, Cristos?'

She held her breath for his answer. He gave it to her immediately. 'No. That wasn't me. The risks I take are informed by business savvy and market awareness as well as gut instinct. I didn't do that Master's degree for nothing.'

She let out her breath on a sigh of relief.

'But it was my father.'

'*What?*' Was there to be one unexpected blow after another?

'He was the kind of gambler that you described. But he wasn't a clever gambler. He lost more than he ever won.'

'Gambling—the sure way to get nothing for something,' she said slowly. 'I don't know where that saying comes from but it seems apt.'

'You're right,' he said. 'But with my kind of gambling I've ended up way ahead.'

'But not your father.' Why hadn't he told her this before? What other secrets were there for him to spill?

'He was also a petty criminal, a grifter. Fraud. Embezzlement. Out and out theft.' Cristos spoke in a matter-of-fact way and she knew it was because he found this 'confession' so difficult. 'That's why he worked to improve his English—it made it easier to target tourists. Ripping off naïve visitors to the Greek islands was his specialty. He was handsome and charming and people believed his schemes and fabrications.'

'Cristos, I'm so sorry.' She reached out her hand to clasp his. 'When did you find out?'

'I think I always knew,' he said. His grip tightened on her hand. 'Was always aware there was something not right about our family. That my *baba* was someone I couldn't boast about like other kids did about their dads.'

Compassion for him swelled in her heart. She imagined him as an adorable little boy, feeling different and alone. 'That must have been tough for you.'

'It was much worse for my mother.'

'I can imagine. How did your mother get involved with him?' His family seemed so traditional, so straight. Now she realised in the time she'd been here no one had ever mentioned Cristos's parents. It was as if they'd been wiped from the family history.

'He was working as a barman in Nidri when he met my mother. He conned her into falling in love with him. By the time she realised what he was, she was pregnant. She married him anyway. Soon after, they had to leave town before the bar owner discovered he'd been cheated of his profits.' He paused and her heart clenched at the anguish on his face. 'We were always having to leave town.'

'You said he was away a lot of the time. I assumed you meant on business.'

'He was in prison,' he said bluntly.

His answer was not totally unexpected, but no less shocking all the same. 'Oh, Cristos. I'm so sorry. How awful for you. And for your mother.'

'Yeah. It was.'

She could see how difficult it was for him to divulge these long-held secrets, revisit unpleasant memories.

'What did your poor mother do?'

'She would try to get work near the prison so she could visit him whenever she could. She was a nurse. Or we would go to live with my grandparents while he was doing his time. My education was interrupted. As I got older, I lived with my grandparents even when he was out so I could have some consistency at school.'

She searched his face, saw all the pent-up pain she had never before recognised. 'Cristos, why didn't you share this with me before?'

He couldn't meet her gaze. 'I was brought up to be ashamed of my father. Not to ever talk about him. To believe that my lovely mother was foolish for loving him. My mother adored him. She always went back to him no matter what. Even though she must have known his promises to change were worthless.' He sighed and Hayley wondered if he was aware of the depth of anguish he revealed. 'Another reason my family hated him is because they think she died of a broken heart after he died. His fault, of course. The diagnosis was a fast-acting cancer but to my grandparents it was because their only daughter couldn't live without her feckless husband.'

'Tragic. And horrible for you to be left without parents.' Was it surprising Penelope was so protective of her grandson? No wonder she'd been averse to hasty marriages with strangers.

Cristos took her other hand so he held both clasped in his. 'Here's the thing. The truth I struggled with as a kid—I loved him too. I couldn't help but love him although I wasn't allowed to admit it. Now I'm admitting it to you. Finally.'

'That's very sad. He was your father...you were a little kid.' In spite of all her mother's idiosyncrasies—including a blatant dislike of Cristos—Hayley loved her mother. Her father too.

'*Baba* was charming and fun and carried you along with him with his grand ideas—like a big kid himself, I suppose. I wanted to believe in him.

Of course, he always disappointed me in the end. He disappointed everyone.'

Hayley thought of how Cristos had struggled to recall any simple father-son moments. No wonder, with a dad in and out of prison for much of his childhood.

'That's such a sad story, Cristos. But you could have told me. I wish you had.'

He raised his head in challenge. 'Would you have married me if you'd known my father was a jailbird?'

'Without question,' she said immediately. 'However, if you'd been the jailbird I might have thought twice.' Even so. From what Cristos had said, his father was very handsome and very charming. Like father, like son. Would she have been any more capable of resisting him than his mother had been unable to resist his father?

'I plead totally innocent on that one,' he said, raising his hand as if swearing an oath. 'My grandparents kept such a close eye on me, terrified I would turn out like my father. Any boyhood naughtiness was firmly jumped on, I assure you.'

Sitting in the bed, with a shaft of morning sun

highlighting his bare shoulders, with his hair all messed and his stubble halfway to a beard, Cristos looked every inch The Sexiest Man in Europe. 'You probably look like him, don't you?'

'Yes. And I am a gambler. I tried to deny that instinct but I couldn't.'

'Though you channel it in a very different way. You also have a highly developed business sense that it seems your father lacked.'

'And an education, which he also lacked. He was determined that I would do well at school. He wanted more for me than he ever had.'

Hayley nodded thoughtfully. 'So he loved you back.'

There was a long pause before Cristos answered. 'I guess he did. So did my mother—she didn't want to leave me, she fought that cancer. And my grandparents care so much. I was lucky.'

She loved him too.

Her heart swelled with a rush of love for him.

She had never stopped loving him.

She wanted to tell him no one loved him more than she did, never had, never would. That while he wanted to protect her, she had always wanted to care for him. But this wasn't the time. If she told him she loved him she would want to kiss him. She would want to cover that handsome, beloved face with kisses, kiss all over his Greek god, perfect body. She knew what that would lead to. There would be no more talk. And they still needed to talk. *She had secrets to share too.*

'So, no one other than me knows about what you call "gambling" and what I would call "astute, high-risk investment strategy"?' She made quote marks with her fingers.

He smiled, white teeth against olive skin; dark, sexy stubble; raven-black hair, and those seductive green eyes. Her heart turned a somersault. Intense desire mixed with intense love—a potent mix.

He was still her husband.

The way she felt right now those divorce papers would never be signed. But she had to be practical. Continue the conversation. See where it led them. They might never get another chance.

'That terminology would be debatable if my grandparents, who feared my turning out like my criminal father, ever found out how I earn my living these days. Playing the stock market, trading, investing in cyber products, is too intangible for them. I got in the habit of never mentioning it.'

'That's why you never thought to mention it to me.'

'That's right.'

'Even though you were doing a deal involving a good deal of our money with a woman who made no secret about wanting you.'

He shook his head. 'She might have wanted me. Be in no doubt that I didn't want her. I made it very clear to her that I wasn't interested, that I loved you.'

'How did she take that?' Hayley still felt nauseous at the thought of the gorgeous-looking woman and her supercilious ways. But also somehow relieved to know she hadn't been imagining Ginny's interest in snagging her husband. She'd had enough other reasons at the time to question her sanity.

'Ginny threatened to pull out of the deal. It was…unpleasant to say the least. I was battling it out with her on the day you lost the baby. It's why I missed your calls. I switched off the phone so I could concentrate on salvaging the deal.'

'You were with her that day? So she wasn't lying.'

He frowned. 'What do you mean?'

'That morning, after you'd left, Ginny called our apartment. To tell you that you'd left your jacket at her hotel room the day before. She spoke to me as if I were the maid but she knew it was me and I got the message she intended. Why was your jacket in her room?'

Cristos cursed. 'I was at a business meeting in the hotel suite she shared with her brother, who'd flown in from San Francisco. I was never alone with her there. I made damn sure of that. My jacket? It was still there when I went back the next day. I was on the point of walking out when thankfully her brother saw sense and the deal went through.'

'To think I tortured myself over her. If you'd just told me—'

'I didn't want to stress you or upset you. Remember, there was a second reason I kept you in the dark.'

She frowned. 'A second reason?' Why did that sound so ominous?

* * *

Cristos chose his words carefully. He dreaded hurting his beautiful, vulnerable wife. 'This is difficult,' he said.

'I don't know what you mean by difficult. But I'm sure I can take it,' she said, obviously puzzled.

'I didn't think you could take it back then. You were too…fragile.'

She frowned. 'What do you mean?'

'You changed after you got pregnant,' he said. 'Really changed. I didn't have any experience of pregnant women. I knew about morning sickness, expected it.' But not that his sweet wife would suddenly turn irrational and aggressive and accusatory in one breath, a sobbing heap in the next.

'I didn't have morning sickness, apart from some initial queasiness.'

'No. But you got very moody.' He knew he had to be extremely careful with his choice of words. 'I never knew what version of Hayley I'd find when I got home.'

She got up abruptly from the bed, took a few steps away from him and then turned back. 'Grumpy, suspicious, paranoid or just plain mean. Is that what you're talking about?'

He jumped up from the bed, wrapped the sheet toga-style around him. They had to be on an equal footing for this kind of conversation. 'I wouldn't put it quite like that,' he said cautiously. But she was right.

Her mouth twisted. 'You're being kind. I was up and down and all over the place. Some days when you weren't coming home I'd cry all day. Other days I stayed in bed unable to get up. I didn't really know what to expect about being pregnant. I thought all that must be normal.'

'*Koukla*, that doesn't sound right. What did your doctor say?' He should have been at the doctor's appointments with her, not away working in another city.

'The lovely *dottoressa* said I was in perfect physical health and all was progressing as it should. She spoke good English but I didn't feel I could tell her about how I was feeling. I figured it was part and parcel of being pregnant. Turns out it wasn't.'

Alarm shot through him. 'What do you mean?'

'That's the gap in the story you wondered about. Now it's my turn to share secrets. I was suffering from depression.'

'You were depressed?' He drew her into his arms, hugged her close. 'Why didn't I know?' He had let her down in so many ways.

She pulled back so she was still in the circle of his arms but could look up at him. Her face was drawn and the blue of her eyes as dull as the sea on a cloudy day. 'I don't want to go over old ground but you weren't there a lot.'

Because he'd become obsessed with accumulating wealth for her and the baby. To be the good Greek provider his father hadn't been. He'd played his cards completely wrong.

'Did the depression have anything to do with the miscarriage?' He didn't really know what were the right questions to ask. He went with asking the ones where he genuinely wanted to hear the answers.

'They don't know. Pre-natal depression is not that common apparently.'

'Pre-natal depression? If you didn't tell the doctor how you were feeling, how do you know that was the diagnosis?'

Her smile was shaky around the edges. 'I'll have to explain backwards.'

'I'm listening,' he said. And not letting her go.

'The day of the miscarriage I woke up feeling terrible, nauseous when I hadn't been feeling nauseous. I had a headache but I didn't want to take any medication. I started a row with you when you asked me what was wrong. You wanted to stay but I insisted you go. Then felt aggrieved you hadn't insisted on staying. I couldn't settle. The phone call from Ginny set me into a spin. Then in the afternoon the cramping started. I was petrified. That's when I called you the first time and kept on calling you. When you didn't answer, I called my mum. When there was blood, I called the ambulance.'

Cristos closed his eyes against the rush of guilt and regret. 'The next time I saw you was in the hospital. You'd lost the baby. I was devastated. Worried sick about you. You looked as white as the hospital sheets. You turned your head on the pillow and closed your eyes. Then mumbled something. I leaned closer. Only to hear you tell me you hated me and to go away.' He'd felt as if he'd been kicked in the gut by a gang of thugs wearing steel-capped boots.

'That was the depression speaking, even then,'

she said in a voice so low it was practically a whisper.

'Then you sat up and shouted for me to leave you alone. I was escorted from the room by two burly wardsmen and not allowed back.' His humiliation and anger was still raw.

'I don't remember,' she said. 'My memories of around that time are very hazy.'

'I was your husband so I had some rights. Eventually I was told you'd been taken in for a procedure. I wouldn't be allowed to see you until the morning—that is, if you gave me your permission.'

'I'm sorry, Cristos.' He hugged her close and she buried her head against his shoulder. 'What did you do?' Her voice was muffled.

'I found a waiting room but got kicked out of it so I went back to the apartment. I didn't sleep. I got back to the ward in the morning to be told you'd been transferred to a private hospital. And you didn't want me to know where.'

'I can only say I'm sorry again,' she said.

'I was frantic with worry about you. But I spoke Italian and understood they believed I was an abusive husband. That perhaps my abuse had something to do with you losing the baby. I half expected to get arrested.'

She groaned. 'That was my parents. They'd flown to Milan after my first phone call. They listened to my delirious garble and thought the worst.'

'Then they spirited you out of the country and I didn't see you again until you turned up here. You can see what I mean about gaps.'

She stood very still in his arms. 'I meant it when I said I don't remember much of that time. I fell into a deep depression, which can, apparently, happen after a miscarriage. But as the weeks went by I didn't pull out of it as the hormones settled. My parents were so worried about me they booked me into a clinic where I was diagnosed and treated. Post-natal depression is relatively common. Not so post-miscarriage depression and pre-natal depression dating right back to the beginning of my pregnancy.'

'Why wasn't I told about this? I should have been there to help you.'

'I'd been told you hadn't tried to see me. I didn't think I was going to get better. And I blamed you.' Her voice caught at the edges.

'But you did get better.'

'Thankfully, with the right treatment and medication. But it took a long time. I was still on the medication when I went to Australia.'

Cristos gritted his teeth. 'And still the husband wasn't told.'

'You know the story of what I did there. How I became the person I wanted to be. Maybe I needed to grow up. Maybe I'd be a better wife now.'

Hope flared. 'What do you mean, "be a better wife"?'

'I was speaking hypothetically,' she said hastily.

'You came here to divorce me,' he said. 'Have you changed your mind?'

She twisted back out of his arms. 'Yes. No. I'm not sure of anything after last night.'

'Could we make our marriage work again?'

She raised her beautiful blue eyes to him and he could see they were still clouded by uncertainty. 'We learned so much about each other this morning. Then there was last night—it meant a lot, Cristos.'

He pulled her back to him, held her so close he could feel her heat through their informal attire of

towel and toga. 'It meant a lot to me too, *koukla*.'
She might still have doubts but he didn't. 'And
I'm sure I want us to be together again.'

'But there's still a lot more to learn. We've
barely scratched the surface. I'm frightened we
might make the same mistakes.'

'You yourself said we were different people.
Surely we've learned from our mistakes. You are
my wife and I don't want to let you go again.
We've got time today to find out everything you
need to give our marriage a second chance.'

He was about to set out a plan of action that
would include more time in that big bed, followed
by some serious discussion about what a shared
future could involve. Then his mobile phone rang.
Alex.

He listened to his cousin. 'I'll be down,' he said
and terminated the call.

'What's happened?' asked Hayley.

Cristos strode over to the balcony doors and
flung first the shutters open and then the doors.
Sunlight streamed in from a blue sky clear but
for a few drifting white clouds. Snow on the tree
canopies sparkled with reflected sunbeams. Beyond was a millpond-calm sea in shades of aqua-

marine and turquoise. A perfect crisp winter's day on Kosmimo.

Cristos cursed under his breath. He would so much have preferred to see choppy, stormy water that would keep Hayley on the island.

He stepped aside. 'You can see for yourself. The storm has blown itself out. No fresh snow has fallen.'

Hayley joined him at the doors to the balcony. 'Does that mean—?'

'There's no reason boats can't leave the island.' His voice was gruff with disappointment.

'And the roads to the airport are open?'

He could lie and say no. But she would find out the truth soon enough. 'I'm sure they're clearing them as we speak.'

'That doesn't necessarily mean I have to leave the island, does it? Not when we've still got so much more to say to each other. Can I stay another day? I don't have to be back at work just yet.'

He swung around to face her, not even attempting to conceal his urgency. He couldn't lose her again. 'Stay, Hayley. Not just for today. Or tomorrow. Stay with me for ever.'

CHAPTER FOURTEEN

HAYLEY LOOKED UP at Cristos, wrapped in a sheet and looking more like a Greek god than ever. 'For ever? Surely it's too soon to talk about for ever. We've only had two days back together.' She wanted him. She loved him. But she needed more time to be certain that she wanted to commit again to a marriage that had ended in so much pain she'd had to flee to the other side of the world.

'Two days? I had more than two years missing you, aching for you. It would kill me if you flew back to Australia. You are the only woman I have ever wanted. Stay here with me as my wife. Make your life with me again, *koukla*.' His eyes narrowed with the sensual, hungry look that made her want to melt back into his arms and forget everything but him. 'This time for ever.'

He drew her to him for a quick kiss that lingered in its deliciousness. He ran his finger down her cheek and traced her lips, swollen with the countless kisses she had enjoyed during a long night of loving. Loving as she knew no other man could ever give her.

He was six feet two of dark-haired, green-eyed temptation enticing her into forgetting everything she'd learned about what she needed while they'd been apart. 'But I have a job in Australia. A good life.' A hard-won life of security and certainty, a private life of answering to no one but herself.

A lonely life with no Cristos to warm her bed and her heart.

'You can have a better life with me,' he said dismissively. 'A new job in Europe.' She'd forgotten how arrogant he could be. How certain he was about the decisions he made. But then he bowed his head. 'I can't lose you again, Hayley.' Along with that arrogance was a hint of uncertainty, of vulnerability, that tugged at her heart. It was one of the reasons she had fallen so deeply in love with him back when they'd been students.

'I don't want to lose you again either.' She was suddenly very sure of that. She had never wanted any man but him. But she had to weigh up the costs of—again—giving up her life for him.

With all the soul searching this morning, she found herself digging deeper into her own motivations. Was this what she'd secretly wanted all along—from the time she'd packed her bag back in Sydney? She hadn't needed to deliver the divorce documents in person—in fact she'd been advised against it. Deep down had she hoped, by her coming to Greece, she and Cristos would rediscover what they'd lost?

That they would fall in love again?

'We've wasted so much time already,' he said. 'Why waste any more spent apart?' His hands rested possessively on her shoulders. 'We were happy at the start. We can be happy again. I guarantee it. Say yes, *Kyria* Theofanis, like you said yes when I asked you to marry me the first time.'

It had been so long since she'd been called *Mrs.* Yes, she wanted to be his wife again. She couldn't risk losing him a second time.

She took a deep breath. Excitement rippled through her. Time to commit. To reclaim the man she loved as her husband. 'Cristos, I want—'

His phone sounded again, its shrill tone intruding on the quiet and privacy of the honeymoon suite. He uttered one of those interesting Greek swear words. 'Alex again. I don't have to answer it to know he wants me downstairs. It must be pandemonium with everyone wanting to get home.'

She frowned. 'Why does he need you? I know he's your cousin and your friend. But surely there are others who can help him.' Wasn't being here with her more important?

'Because I'm co-owner of the resort. I'm as much responsible for whatever is happening as he is.'

Hayley struggled to get enough air to fill her lungs. This was a multimillion-euro property. 'Since when?'

'I invested in Pevezzo Athina early, when it was just a dream in Alex's hotelier heart. It's an investment that's paid off handsomely already.'

'Why didn't you tell me?'

More secrets.

'We hadn't had the opportunity to have the money conversation yet.'

'What do you mean? You said you were comfortable. But you must be more than comfortable to be able to afford a place like this.'

'You could say that. Dell likes to call me the secret millionaire. Multimillionaire is a more apt description. As my wife, you won't have to worry about money ever again, *koukla*.'

She stepped back to release his hands from her shoulders. 'Were you testing me? Keeping your millions out of the equation in case they swayed my decision to reconcile with you?'

He frowned. 'Of course not. Why would you think that? My fortune is not something I boast about but I wasn't trying to hide anything from you. I was lucky to be in at the beginning of exciting new developments—shopping apps and transport-sharing apps, pretty-much-anything-sharing apps. The internet couldn't get enough of them back then. I sold my initial investments at the top of the market.'

His phone rang again. Then again. And again. He scowled. 'I have to get down there. Just to see what's so urgent. Don't go anywhere, Hayley. Stay here. Please. I'll be back.'

She was too shocked to say anything other than yes. She watched as he hastily dressed in the clothes she had wrestled off him last night and tossed on the floor.

More secrets and lies.

She'd thought he'd spilled all his truths the night

before. She had nothing more to lay on the table. But not her husband.

Her multimillionaire husband.

What else hadn't he told her?

'Kiss me, Hayley. I know the bank balance comes as a shock. But not a bad kind of shock, right? Remember how skint we were when we were first together?'

'It just takes some getting used to.'

'Everything I've done was for you, *koukla*. And without you, I'm worth nothing. Not a cent, penny or *lepton.*'

She rose up on tiptoe to kiss him on his mouth. Even that swift touch made her shudder with pleasure. His eyes darkened and he returned the kiss, hard and possessive. 'I'll call you on that kiss when I get back,' he said, his voice deep and husky and laden with promise.

He slammed the door shut behind him. Hayley heard his footsteps disappear down the marble corridor towards the stairs. In a daze, she looked around the room. The rumpled sheets. Her silk pyjamas discarded on the floor. His glass of water on the table beside the bed. An empty bottle of health drink from the fridge. He'd joked he needed to restore his stamina after their third—or was it their fourth?—bout of lovemaking. She'd insisted on sharing it because she'd needed the stamina too. His scent—their mingled scents—hung in the air. The room already had the familiar scent of the rooms they'd shared during their married life. It echoed with his absence.

She was back in that tiny apartment in Milan. Cristos off at work doing his thing, her left on her own, kept out of the picture. Pushed firmly right back down on the lowest rungs of the decision-making perch. Once again she felt like that little brown peahen pecking away at her life in the shadow of her glamorous peacock husband. Nothing had changed. *He* hadn't changed.

But she had. Back with Cristos, it would be too easy to lose herself again. Now she was used to a different life. A life she'd fought hard for, where she sat proudly on the top perch when it came to determining how she lived it. Had Cristos grown too rich and powerful to ever want to share it with her? Too used to having his own way? She couldn't go back there. And the longer she stayed with him, the more difficult it would be to leave.

There would be a boat going back to Nidri this

morning. She needed to get down to the dock so she could be among the first to leave the island.

It would take her five minutes to pack everything she had into her handbag. She would take only what she'd come with. Even Dell's pink dress and the beautiful shoes from Penelope she would leave behind. She wanted nothing that would remind her of her time on Kosmimo.

As Cristos had predicted, it was chaos downstairs with everyone who wanted to get off the island determined to be in the first boat. He'd got immediately caught up in it, especially as he was not only a co-owner of the resort, but also captain of a boat with the capacity to carry a good number of passengers.

He wished he'd brought Hayley down with him to help. After all, she would have a stake in the resort too. Not to mention a calm, efficient manner. Then the truth of what he'd done hit him with the impact of a sledgehammer. He totally ignored a friend of Alex's who was demanding to be first on board. Why the hell had he left Hayley back up in that room by herself? As he'd done back in Milan. He cursed himself under his breath for his stupidity. Only it couldn't have been under his breath as the guy he was dealing with took offence and kicked up a stink about his rudeness.

He didn't care. The only thing to concern him was what an idiot he'd been. Hayley hadn't even said yes to his new proposal and he'd slid right back into the behaviour that had driven her from him. He understood now that it wasn't just the day she'd lost the baby that he'd let her down. It was also the build-up to that day, as he had so relentlessly pursued a policy for the future without consulting her. What had she said about being booted off the perch?

He had to get back up to that room. Apologise. Grovel. And explain how different things would be if she took him back. How they would go back to the equal partnership that had started their marriage. When they'd been happy.

But she wasn't in the room. Her jeans, her sweatshirt and the pink dress were neatly folded on the bed. Everything she'd acquired on the island, in fact, was still in the room. Her blue coat and her smart boots were gone from the closet. Of course she could have gone outside to wave goodbye to the guests departing the island. But the echoing emptiness of the room didn't suggest that. He took the marble stairs two at a time.

He checked the common areas downstairs. No Hayley. There were still a good number of people milling about. Including Arianna, who immediately approached him. 'Are you looking for your wife?' asked Arianna.

'Yes,' he said shortly, not trusting himself to say more to the spiteful woman who had been so rude to Hayley.

'I saw her heading down to the dock with the others leaving on the boat to Nidri. She was all dressed up to go. Sorry it didn't work out with you two.' She didn't sound sorry at all.

Cristos brushed past her without a further word, not caring if she thought him ill-mannered. He didn't want this woman on Kosmimo or anywhere near him. If Penelope wanted him to fix things with Hayley, she could get Arianna out of their hair. Not that he needed his grandparent's urging to fix things with his wife. He'd made that decision all on his own. And then totally stuffed up the execution of it.

He ran down the steps that led to the bay, heedless of the puddles of melting snow. Immediately he saw Hayley, not waiting on the dock with the others, but sitting a good distance away to the side on a rustic bench Alex had placed there because it was such a pleasant place to sit in summer. It seemed a lonely place to be in winter.

The Ionian Sea stretched out ahead of her, the wooded hills of the island behind. She looked small and vulnerable in the landscape, and very alone. Cristos fisted his hands beside him. He could tell by the slump of her shoulders and her stillness that she was hurting.

His fault.

She shouldn't be sitting there alone and melancholy. They had wasted too many years apart. She should be with him, cherished and loved and making a new life together. But it seemed he still had some work ahead of him to convince her of that.

He didn't immediately alert her to his presence, just took the moments before she would sense he was there to observe her.

She was wearing the blue coat he'd bought her back in Italy from a favourite designer he'd walked for at Milan Fashion Week. He'd thought it would be perfect for his lovely wife. But Hayley hadn't been as excited about the expensive gift as he'd thought. She had only just had her pregnancy confirmed and hadn't been showing at all but she might already have been suffering from depression.

Was she depressed now? With her head bowed she certainly looked it. But what did he know about depression? Only that it meant more than just feeling down sometimes, that it was an illness. No matter, he would love and cherish her all the more.

She needed him.

He cleared the distance to the bench. She must have heard him but she didn't turn around. 'May I sit next to you, Lady in Blue?' he asked, not taking anything for granted.

She nodded wordlessly, shuffled along to make room for him. She was wearing not just the coat, but also the trousers, sweater and boots she'd worn the day she'd arrived on the island. Her travelling outfit. Her hands were clasped together on her lap. He noticed she was only wearing one of her fine leather gloves on her right hand. Her rings were still on her bare left hand, he noted with relief.

'You're only wearing one glove,' he said. 'Isn't your other hand cold?'

'One of the goats ate the other one when I was helping Penelope put them away before the storm.' She gave a watery smile.

Her answer was so not what he'd expected that he laughed. '*Koukla*, you always surprise me.' He wanted to reach out and take her cold little hand and warm it between his. But her body language screamed, *Don't touch!*

'What are you doing here?' he asked.

'Thinking about my next step.'

'All by yourself? I'd hoped your next step would be taken with me,' he said.

'So did I.' She heaved a great sigh. When she turned to face him he saw her eyes were red-rimmed. He felt gutted that he had upset her.

'You haven't changed,' she said. 'If I went back to you it would be more of the same. You ruling the roost, me clucking along below with never a compromise from you.'

'That's not true. I have changed, even if I didn't show it this morning by leaving you in the hotel room. But how much more honest could I have been with you last night and this morning? I shared things with you that I've never told anyone.'

'I appreciate that. But would you ever make a life decision that was about what I wanted? I want to be with you, Cristos, make no mistake about that. But it means giving up my life again. You want me to throw away everything I've achieved in Sydney, my career, my prospects, to stay here with you. I'd be as miserable as I was in Milan.'

'It doesn't have to be that way,' he said. 'We could work out a way to be together that suits us both.'

Her chin tilted upward; her eyes challenged him. 'What if you came with me to Australia?'

'That's a great idea. I've always wanted to visit Sydney, see where Alex and Dell came from, the restaurant my great-uncle started. I could easily live there with you.'

'Really? What about your work?'

'I can run my business anywhere there's WiFi and an international airport. I just want to be with you, living as husband and wife. I honestly don't care wherever that might be in the world.'

Now he did take her bare hand. It was icy cold and he rubbed it between his own much larger hands. 'We only started to talk about this a few hours ago. As you said, we've still got a way to go.'

She caught his hand and closed hers over his. 'I'm sorry I doubted you. I hope you're not having second thoughts about me.'

'Never. Not since the day we pledged to spend our lives together.'

She turned her face for his kiss. It was short and very sweet, a kiss of comfort and confirmation. He could carry on kissing her all morning but there was more that needed to be said.

'There's something else I want to tell you,' he said. 'One more thing my family keeps hidden because of the shame.'

She raised her brows. 'About your father?'

'My father died in prison.'

'Cristos, no. I'm so sorry. Did he…end his own life?'

'Nothing like that,' he said. 'He died in prison on the day he was due to be released. In a fight, protecting a younger inmate in a notoriously overcrowded and understaffed hell-hole.'

She gasped and her grip on his hands tightened. 'So it was an honourable death.'

'Yes. He died with honour, although that was no consolation to us. My mother and I were waiting outside for him to come through those prison gates. I was holding a balloon saying "welcome home Dad". We waited for hours but he never came. When eventually we were told what had happened, that's when I—a thirteen-year-old boy—saw the moment my mother's heart broke. Not for all the wrongs he did to us and to others. Not for when he had stolen money from her purse to place a bet on a "sure thing". Or purloined my pocket money. But when she realised she would never see him again—the man she adored.'

'And you?' Her voice broke.

'That's when I vowed that no woman I ever loved would go through what my mother went through. My wife would be honoured and cherished and want for nothing. That was my only motivation in our marriage—to look after you. I made mistakes and I'm sorry for them. But everything I did, the modelling, the investments, the risk taking was for us. To secure our future. And the future of our children. More than anything I want our futures to be spent together.'

'Oh, Cristos, I don't know what to say.' Tears glistened on her lashes.

He cupped her chin in one hand, gently wiped away the tears with his other. 'That's what Greek men do. We protect our women. We look after our families. It's in our blood. Don't say anything, except that you'll stay.'

She blinked away the remaining tears. 'Before I do, there's one more thing. Not a secret, a worry. You mentioned children.'

He nodded. 'You know I want a family with you.'

'Me too,' she said. 'I long to have your baby. But I'm petrified of getting pregnant again. The depression was so frightening. Both during the pregnancy and afterwards.'

'You're quite over the depression now?'

'Yes, thank heaven.'

'What do the doctors say? Is it likely to happen again with another pregnancy?'

'They can't predict how my hormones will react. The depression might strike, it might not.'

'That's simple, then. We won't have children. It's not worth it if you—'

She put up her hand to stop him. 'No. I'm prepared to take the risk. But not if it would be like last time. I can't be left on my own to cope with it.' Her mouth twisted. 'Or not cope as I did then.'

He put his hands on her shoulders to reassure her. 'It would be very different next time. I work from home. I would always be there for you when you needed me.'

'Thank you,' she said. 'I mean, it might not happen but if it did, if I—'

'Whatever does or does not happen, I would be there for you. We're a partnership.'

He put his arm around her shoulder and they both sat looking out to sea. Silence hung between them. Slowly he became aware of the sounds of the small waves swishing on the beach, the wind rustling through the trees, chatter and laughter from the direction of the dock. He was aware of the sound of his own breathing, his heart thudding against his chest.

'Why did you really come down here?' he said. 'Just to think or were you planning to take the boat to Nidri?'

'Yes,' she said. Again he felt that kick to the gut so he felt like doubling over with the pain.

'I felt like nothing had changed. After all we'd

gone through, I'd be signing up for the same relationship that had ended in so much pain and regret,' she said, her voice unsteady. 'I thought my only option was to go through with the divorce. My plan was to leave the divorce papers in the room for you to find after I'd gone with a note asking you to sign and return them to the lawyer.'

'I didn't see any divorce papers there. Did you hide them somewhere or—?'

'I didn't leave them. And I didn't ask for a place on the boat. I realised running away wasn't going to solve anything—like it didn't last time. It would have been a stupid, childish thing to do. And this time I didn't have a depressive illness to blame my behaviour on. Difficult as I might find it, I had to do the grown-up thing and confront you. Talk about what we both expected from a reconciliation. See if we could make it work.' She looked away. 'Sorry, long speech.'

'A speech I'm glad I heard. Glad you stuck around to deliver it. Although I would have followed you, you know. All the way to Sydney. I had no intention of letting you go again.'

'I'm glad I didn't make you chase me all that way.' But the curve of her smile told him she was delighted that he would have done so. 'I'll look forward to us travelling back together and starting our new life.'

'Do you have any more questions? Have I explained myself well enough?'

'Very satisfactory answers. No more questions.' Her voice hitched. 'Because the main reason I didn't leave was that I simply couldn't bear to be away from you. Two mornings of waking up next to you made me know I wanted to be there with you for the rest of our lives.' She sniffed.

Cristos wished he could do the chivalrous thing men did in movies and offer her a big snowy white linen handkerchief. But the best he had to offer was an oil-soaked cloth from the boat, which he doubted would be appreciated so he left it in his pocket.

She lifted her face to his. 'Because I love you, Cristos. I never stopped loving you. I think I came to this island in the first place subconsciously hoping I might find you still loved me too.'

'And you found I had never stopped loving you, not for a minute. I love you, Hayley. There has only ever been you. The years apart were torture for me. When I saw you at the church on Saturday I thought you'd come back to me. My spirits soared. When you talked divorce you drove me to my lowest point. I can only thank the forces of nature that conjured up a storm to keep you here until you changed your mind.'

'Being with you is what changed my mind, not the weather,' she said. 'My wonderful, wonderful man.'

A burst of cheering erupted from the people on the dock. Startled, Cristos looked up to see the boat they'd booked to pick up the guests was heading toward the dock.

'Do you know why they're so excited about going back?' Hayley asked.

'Because they're sick of being trapped on the island?'

'Because it's Valentine's Day. I'd forgotten.'

'Of course, it's February the fourteenth,' he said. 'Valentine's Day is a big deal in Greece. The whole Cupid's arrow thing started here. Only it belonged to Eros, the god of love in ancient Greek mythology. The ancient Romans called him Cupid. Greeks do like to get loved up on Valentine's Day.' He felt that arrow still in his heart, only now it would stay lodged there for the rest of his life. He would never, ever let Hayley go again.

'So it's a good day for a reconciliation?' she said.

'It's an excellent day for a reconciliation. Because in Greece Valentine's Day is not just about romantic love, it's also about forgiveness. Will you forgive me, Hayley? Because without forgiveness, without letting go of the past, we won't be able to go forward.'

'Of course I forgive you. If you can forgive me for hiding from you. I didn't realise how much I hurt you. And I guess I have to forgive myself for that.'

'Clean slate, then?' he said.

She nodded. 'I just want to be your wife again. No pretence. No secrets. I want you to be my husband again. Looking after me, but letting me look after you too.'

'We can celebrate February the fourteenth each year as the anniversary of our new marriage.'

'You mean we get to celebrate two anniversaries each year?'

'Why not? Both days are special. And you get two lots of presents.'

'What could there possibly be to complain about that?' she said, laughing. 'I love you, husband.'

'I love you, wife.'

He helped her up from the bench with an arm around her. 'C'mon, *koukla*. Let's go start our new life together.'

EPILOGUE

Fifteen months later

HAYLEY STOOD OUTSIDE the little white chapel perched on the edge of a white limestone cliff on Kosmimo. The sea ahead of her was the most glorious turquoise imaginable, a lone sailboat tacking across the horizon. There wasn't a cloud in the deep blue sky and the late spring sun glistened on the water and warmed her skin through her long white lace dress. The air was fresh with the tang of salt and the scent of the herbs that grew wild on the island.

She and Cristos had just had their photo taken and were waiting for the photographer to organise the next one. Hayley turned to Cristos. 'This is how I always imagined a Greek island to be.'

'It's good to be home,' he said with a deep sigh of satisfaction.

He lifted their four-month-old son, Damianos—

named after Cristos's father in the Greek tradition—to show him the view. 'This is your heritage, *ogios mou*, my son—paradise.' Their beautiful baby boy chuckled, which seemed the appropriate joyful response.

She and Cristos had left Sydney behind them to come back to Europe, to be closer to their families. They were living in his apartment in Athens, but Hayley thought they would probably settle somewhere in London. She had worked right up to a month before the baby was born but wasn't thinking of finding another engineering role until Damianos was at least a year old.

Thankfully, her pregnancy had gone smoothly without a hint of depression except the brief burst of the hormonally induced 'baby blues' that had hit her a few days after the birth and had just as quickly disappeared.

Cristos had been lovingly supportive all the way through and had been with her at the birth. They had both cried as he'd first held his son in his arms, and vowed to be a good father. The baby had black hair and blue eyes and promised to be every bit as handsome as the daddy who adored him.

The last time she'd stood here was in the winter chill and she'd been an outsider. This time the visit to the chapel was for her and Cristos to renew their vows, have their marriage blessed and for the christening of their son.

At last their respective families were getting the celebration they felt they had been cheated of by their hasty register office wedding. Hayley was dressed as a bride in a simple white dress of heavy lace with sweet-scented freesias and apple blossom twisted through her hair. Around her neck was a pendant of a single large tear-shaped sapphire surrounded by diamonds and set in platinum. She had refused to replace her original humble sapphire engagement ring that she cherished for something more elaborate befitting her multimillionaire status. The necklace had been Cristos's gift instead.

The ceremony had gone without a hitch. Little Damianos had howled at being anointed with oil and immersed in water by the priest but had quickly recovered with cuddles from his female relatives, who fought to be the one to comfort him.

He had even been well behaved through all the

photos but, like his father, was beginning to grizzle. The photographer had better be quick with the final group photo before their precious baby erupted into hungry howls.

'How many more photos, Lady in White?' Cristos grumbled. 'This is beginning to feel like work for me. Pose, smile, pose, smile. It's taking me right back to my modelling days.'

'Just this one final family shot,' she said. 'It will be worth it.'

At last they were all assembled. She and Cristos stood at the centre with Damianos—who her mother insisted on calling Damian 'as, after all, he is half English'—in his father's arms. They were flanked by the baby's godparents, Dell and Alex, with their two children; his doting Greek great-grandparents; his equally doting grandparents and aunt from England; and his great-aunt from Australia, who'd been so supportive of Hayley during her pregnancy and Damianos's birth. Her family. She couldn't imagine being happier—especially with the husband she loved more and more each day by her side.

She smiled once more for the camera—she had unlimited smiles today, fuelled by the intense joy bubbling through her. The day brought back memories of her wedding in Durham, of her first visit to this island bearing documents for a divorce she'd never really wanted, but most of all of the perfectly wonderful times with her husband once they'd put the unhappy times behind them.

Her tiny son continued to give his best gummy smiles to the camera. But abruptly he'd had enough. His little face screwed up and he wailed, a surprisingly loud sound for one so small.

'He's hungry. Hand him over to me,' Hayley said to Cristos. She took the precious bundle into her arms. Her exquisite dress had been designed by a dressmaker friend of Penelope's to suit a nursing mother. Now she and Cristos took their baby to a private spot at the back of the chapel so she could discreetly feed him.

She sat with her baby making sweet little snuffling sounds and her husband's protective arm around her. Cristos kissed her, a brief gentle kiss. 'I have never felt happier, *koukla*,' he said.

'Me neither,' she said. 'This is the happiest day of my life. But then I thought yesterday was the happiest, and the day before that. And I know tomorrow will be even happier as it will be one more day with you.'

He kissed her again. 'Do you realise this now makes three anniversaries for us to celebrate each year?'

'All the better to bind our little family together,' she said.

'Doesn't the love we have for each other, for our son, do that?'

'You're absolutely right,' she said, looking up into his eyes and thinking again how incredibly blessed she was to be married to this man.

* * * * *